Maia's REDEMPTION

Riana La Fleur

Maia's Redemption is dedicated to God, the Author of all stories.

To Brian-Lee, you were a flame that lit so many ablaze. You called the mighty out of the meek and for that, I thank you.

To Paul, you are my creative sounding-board, pre-editing editor and my biggest encourager. I love you forever.

Acknowledgments

It takes a village to publish a book and mine, though small, packs a powerful punch! A huge thank you to my publisher Shaniqua Forde at Shelev Publishing for going above and beyond to ensure we got this book out in record time and for the amazing job you did creating the cover. You are talented and efficient and I couldn't possibly thank you enough!

To my editor Theastarr Valerie, thank you for being as detailed and thorough as any great editor should be. Your patience and commitment to preserving the uniqueness of my voice was greatly appreciated!

It's easy to start writing a book but it takes mettle, consistency and perseverance to complete a manuscript. To the superwomen who pushed me to finish what I started, your encouragement gave me the bursts of motivation I needed to finish the race. To Malissa, Shaniqua, Jacinth & Tao, 'thank you' is not enough but I hope for now, it will do.

Lastly, to all my friends and family, I'm not able to mention you by name because you are so many. However, I want to say thank you for all of your support and love.

Chapter 1

There are moments in life that are unequivocally divine, moments when time and fortune conspire to bring you everything you didn't know you could wish for. Such a moment is usually preceded by a series of remarkable coincidences, culminating in some kind of life-changing encounter. In fact, many recipients of such favor, confess to having a sixth sense, an unexplainable "*knowing*" that something significant was about to happen. That was not the case for Maia Miller. The day that everything changed, felt altogether ordinary.

That serendipitous Sunday found her sitting in a crowded church sanctuary as the pastor spoke about the importance of community. Her eyes were fixed on the enormous projector screen at the front of the large auditorium. The founder of the megachurch was speaking emphatically, but Maia's mind was a million miles away. He'd made a valid point about how Jesus had sent His disciples out in twos to preach the gospel, but Maia hadn't heard much after that. It had been a minute since she'd set foot in a church. However, she had promised herself when she moved to Turnpeake, Texas, four months ago, that she wasn't bringing her past with her. This was a fresh start and she reminded herself daily that the mess she'd left back in Jacksonville was no longer her burden to bear.

After settling into her downtown apartment, Maia had made it her mission to find a home church to attend (preferably somewhere in her neighborhood). This was her first church visit since she'd moved and the nearest one to her apartment. The convenience of a five-minute drive had given her the little push she'd needed to actually make the effort to attend the eight o'clock service. God knows she usually didn't rouse from sleep until at least ten on Sundays. Perhaps that was why she found it difficult to focus today. Reining her scattered thoughts back in, she focused once again on the preacher.

"I challenge you with this…" he continued. "The reason you're scared to connect with people again isn't because people are no good. Can I tell you a secret?"

The silence in the auditorium was now deafening as he let his words hang in the air. Maia's heart felt like it was knocked off kilter, its beat staggering as if trying to remember the rhythm it had danced to all her life. Could he be about to give her the answer to her current predicament?

Ever since leaving Jacksonville, Maia had felt the disconnect between her heart and mind, often feeling like she was outside of herself looking in. She was capable of making judgments, but feelings… true deep emotional connections, didn't seem like a possibility anymore. The pastor's voice once again tugged at her ears.

"You're scared. You're scared that *these* people will hurt you just like *those* people did. But what if, just maybe, these people aren't those people. There are God-sent ones waiting to show you that all people aren't the same. There's life after pain, beloved. There's joy after hurt and it's only found in one place: at the cross. It's found in forgiveness and the courage to trust again. Jesus forgave you. Will you also forgive those who hurt you?"

The band began a slow melody as the worship team sang a popular hymn about trusting Jesus. Maia quickly wiped the unwelcomed tears from her eyes and folded her arms as the preacher asked the courageous ones to stand for prayer. She wasn't one of them. Forgiveness? She wasn't capable of it yet. These wounds were far too fresh to forget. Maybe one day she'd forgive, but today was not that day.

Her thoughts drifted to Mimi and how horribly they parted ways. She quelled the small part of her that still longed for her grandmother's sharp tongue and warm hugs.

When it came down to the wire, Mimi had proven that she'd believe just about anyone over her own flesh and blood. The anger that often threatened to overwhelm Maia rose in her heart again, but she refused to let it take over. What happened in Florida would stay in Florida.

"Excuse me, baby." Maia's eyes darted up to find the owner of the seasoned Texas drawl. She looked about seventy-five, her heavy-set cocoa-colored frame, covered in doily lace. Maia smiled and shifted her legs to allow the older woman to pass freely. She shuffled past Maia, her feet dragging almost as much as her words. "Thank you, beautiful. Have a blessed Sundee now!"

Maia laughed a *thank you* and wished her the same. Maybe she'd visit this church again. Maybe. Sometime during her internal monologue, the preacher had finished his prayer and ended the service. A long trail of people now shuffled behind the matronly Madear who had called her beautiful, so she remained seated, in no hurry to face the daunting mess of traffic that would be sure to fill the church's parking lot.

The former high school auditorium was still packed with people, shuffling through endless rows of seats to make their way to the exit. Maia pulled her phone out of her purse to check the time and write a list for when she stopped by the farmer's market after church.

Time flew by and before she knew it, the loud murmur of voices that filled the arena had turned to alarming silence. How long had she been writing that list? The auditorium looked a lot bigger now that it was empty. She got up from her seat on the far east side and hurriedly made her way down the steps to the lower level. As she walked out into the open area at the front of the stage, she stared in amazement at what God had built through one man's obedience. She'd read about the church's history online and now she saw with her own eyes what God could make out of one man's submission. She recalled the information she'd read...

Pastor Carl and his wife had started this church in their living room with only a vision and a word from God that it would save generations.

She admired that kind of faith and wondered if she'd ever have the courage to do something as wildly brave and equally insane as that.

Maia suddenly felt God tugging at her heart. She felt His conviction before she heard the still, small voice of His Spirit.

"Forgive, Maia. Forgive and I will do the impossible for you."

Tears welled in her eyes again and she pushed her dark curls away from her face in frustration and let the tears flow in earnest. "How?" she screamed and the sound echoed in the empty space. She knelt and let the pain of everything that had happened pour out of her in the only expression she had: tears. "You have to help me. I can't do this anymore. Help me, please." It was all she could manage. Her past was like a dark cloud hovering over her and as much as she tried to move on, its presence was daunting, even hundreds of miles away from the reality of it.

"I'll forgive. Help me to forgive. Help me to feel Your joy again."

"Forget the former things; do not dwell on the past. See, I am doing a new thing! Now it springs up; do you not perceive it?" The whisper filled her with awe and wonder that God would give her a fresh start after everything she'd done.

Looking around the vast empty space, Maia wiped the tears from her eyes. Despite everything that had led her to this moment, she knew without a shadow of a doubt, that it was exactly where she was meant to be. An all-encompassing peace filled her heart despite all the "unknowns" of her future.

Chapter 2

━━ ⋅ ✦ ⋅ ━━

"Miss?" The smooth but strong greeting pulled Maia from her thoughts and she turned to see who spoke.

He looked about thirty with skin the color of some exotic caffeine blend. His black t-shirt and matching jeans made him look more ominous than he probably would have on an ordinary day. Maia was sure her eyes gave her fright away. She scanned the area hoping to find someone, anyone who could possibly protect her from this potential danger.

Mr. Dark and Dangerous seemed to sense her unease and quickly spoke up, "I'm so sorry to interrupt, but they're getting ready to close up."

The man extended a hand to her and she hesitated for a second too long before accepting his help. Gently grasping her outstretched hand, his other hand cupped her elbow. Maia awkwardly struggled to her feet. The extra weight she had packed on since moving to Texas, made it difficult to maneuver. Maybe the stretchy white pencil skirt she wore today was not the best idea, but it was the only thing she'd brought from Florida that still fit. That and the billowy pink blouse she paired with it, were her only possible clothing choices for church. Hence, she now gracelessly struggled to stand in her almost skin-tight get up.

When her feet were finally stable on the floor, the man released her hand and she looked up to get a close-up view of the stranger. He must be security, she concluded, because there was no other reason why anyone's physical presence should be this intimidating. He was at least 6' 3" give or take an inch and she knew this because she was 5' 9", yet he towered over her. From this distance she could see that his eyes matched his mocha skin, their wide, almond shape lending a hint of softness to otherwise chiseled features. He smiled as she examined his features, and immediately he looked a hundred times less dangerous. His eyes crinkled at the corners as he held out his hand.

"I'm sorry, I should have introduced myself first. I'm Derek. I play the bass," he said, giving a slight nod toward the massive elevated platform.

She hesitated before taking hold of his extended hand. "Maia Miller," she responded curtly.

"Nice to meet you, Maia. I'm sorry again by the way. Are you waiting for a ride? Do you need one?"

Maia's eyes narrowed. She wasn't about to stand here and play twenty-one questions with this bass-playing giant and she definitely wasn't going anywhere with him.

"No. I'm fine thanks. I drove," she clipped. If her tone wasn't enough, certainly her expression conveyed annoyance.

"There's a shuttle for the congregants, that's why I asked."

"Oh." Maia bit her lip, looking slightly abashed. They stood in awkward silence for a few seconds before Derek spoke again.

"Well, I'm sorry for keeping you. You have a great day now, Maia." He flashed another easy smile.

"Thank you. Same to you."

Derek turned and walked briskly to a small door next to the stage. He glanced back at her, giving one last nod before disappearing from view.

Maia released a shaky breath, instantly deciding that she didn't like the man. Something about him set off alarm bells inside of her. Maia wasn't sure if it was intuition or the fact that the last handsome church musician she met had utterly and completely shattered her heart.

She allowed only a flicker of a thought before pushing unwelcomed memories of Eli from her mind. Maia seldom even allowed his name into her thoughts, far less memories of him. Shaking her head emphatically to clear her thoughts, she walked as quickly as she could towards the exit. When she finally made it out into the hot summer air, she took a deep breath and appreciated yet again, the peace she felt in Turnpeake.

Looking around the large parking lot, her eyes quickly found her beat up old pickup: Ginger. The truck's faded red paint stood out like a sore thumb among the remaining cars in the lot. She tugged the door a few times before it finally gave an alarming creak and opened. Maia desperately needed a new car, but Ginger would have to do for now… at least until she could save enough to buy something else.

After three failed attempts, Maia clumsily climbed into the driver's seat and began the short trip to the farmer's market. She usually wasn't able to buy everything she wanted, but she never went hungry and for that she was grateful. Things would get better eventually. They had to.

"I met someone at church today," Derek stated casually, leaning against the large bookcase in his father's home office. They'd been chatting for a while about everything and nothing as his dad reviewed the contract for a new building they were buying across town. Derek's last confession however, caused him to abandon the paperwork he had been focusing on and give his full attention to his son.

"Well, don't make me have to ask. Out with it! Who is she?" Pastor Carl was not a curious man, but his current expression spoke plainly of his intrigue.

"I didn't mean 'I met someone, *met someone*'. She was just visiting, I believe, but we chatted for a bit. I don't know, there was just something…different about her." Derek shoved his hands in his pockets. This conversation was way out of his comfort zone. He didn't even know why he'd brought it up in the first place, but he couldn't get the fiery, dark-haired beauty out of his mind.

Derek immediately regretted bringing her up. He knew this was crazy. Just from their short meeting, he could find at least ten reasons why he shouldn't be giving this a second thought. Yet here he was, hours later, trying to shake this "knowing" he had deep in his spirit, that they would meet again. He pushed away from the bookcase and pulled his hands from his pockets.

"It's nothing," Derek quipped, trying to shrug it off.

His father chuckled. "Clearly, it's not 'nothing'. I haven't heard you mention a girl since you and Phil Johnson's youngest daughter split up. And you were what, sixteen then? Tell me about this girl that has you smitten."

Carl took his simple, square-framed spectacles from his face and laid them on his large, mahogany desk. His salt and pepper hair always reminded Derek that his father's wisdom was hard-fought and he could trust his old man's advice.

"It's nothing. She's probably married or engaged, but more than that, she's very much pregnant."

For a second, Derek truly thought he'd have to call 911. He visibly saw Carl struggling to breathe, his Adam's apple doing a haphazard dance in his throat as he tried to regain his composure. Derek watched as several emotions flitted across his father's face before he finally settled on worry.

"Are you okay?" Carl retorted. Derek saw the concern on his father's face and knew where this was going. "I know you've been under a lot of pressure lately, especially since we spoke about my retirement. Do you need to talk to someone?"

Derek released a heavy sigh, refusing to even entertain the thought that there might be some truth to what his dad was saying. "I'm fine, dad. Maybe I just need some sleep. It's about time I head home, anyway. I forgot to put some food out for Zeke. He's probably ripping my house to shreds right now."

"D, I'm sure the dog will be fine. I'm worried about you. I understand that you're under pressure, but a-a pregnant and potentially married woman? That's very unlike you."

"You have it all wrong. I'm not interested in her. I just… Something tells me she's going to be more than a stranger to me. I'm not crazy. You know I'd never date a married woman," he replied, his body tense from the awkward conversation they were having. "I'm gonna head out and go feed Zeke."

"Okay son, but if you need someone to talk to, I'm here."

"Thanks dad," he said, tapping the bookcase lightly before he turned and left the office. He shut the door behind him and made up his mind not to waste any more time on futile thoughts.

It was time to go home, feed his dog, and get his mind off of everything else that tumbled around in his head… including the beautiful stranger he met and the fact that his father had asked him to take over a church of over five thousand congregants. Derek was done thinking for the day.

Walking briskly to his car, he jumped into the black '96 Camaro and started for home. He'd think about these things another time, but for now he would rest his weary mind.

Chapter 3

Later that week, Maia sat in a slightly tattered rocking chair; its wooden frame chipped in many places. It was pretty much a hazard, but she loved it. It was the only piece of furniture she'd brought from Jacksonville and the only thing that brought her comfort in her new apartment. The chair was the only gift she'd ever gotten from her mother. It was her sixteenth birthday and that day, ten years ago, was the last time she'd seen her mom.

After a long week of work, Maia was grateful for the reprieve of Friday. She used her toes to revive the rocking motion of the chair again and gently rubbed her baby bump. Nothing calmed her baby girl like this rocking chair and a lullaby. Nights like this, oversized pajamas donned, and rocking chair in full swing, were the only times Maia still sang. Tonight, Lily's lullaby was one of Maia's favorite old hymns. She sang quietly, hoping that her daughter could feel the love that seemed to be a living, breathing thing in her chest ever since she'd seen that pregnancy test twenty-two weeks ago. Maia hit a high note, defaulting to a wispy falsetto. Lily gave a hard punch to her navel in response.

Maia winced and chuckled at the same time. "Guess you're not a fan of mommy's falsetto, huh?" She wished she could put into adequate words the love she felt for her daughter, but words didn't suffice. "Mommy loves you baby girl... more than you could ever know."

She looked around her tiny apartment. It was barely big enough for one person, far less, her *and* a baby. She'd had a long, hard week at work and her back now ached a little from standing all day at the coffee shop, but she thanked the Lord in her heart. If Sarah, the shop owner, hadn't taken a liking to her and given her a job as a barista, she'd be homeless right now. This tiny sublet was more than a blessing. It was a miracle. She knew she'd need another source of income if she was going to be ready for Lily's arrival though. The few items she was able to afford after bills and ob/gyn visits, only scratched the surface of things she needed before her daughter was born. Maia sighed loudly, overwhelmed.

"Trust Me." The still, small voice of God interrupted her worrying and her breath caught.

"Lord, I trust You. I know You will come through for me," she whispered in the quiet, a tear escaping her eye and dripping onto her yellow pajama top. "Oh Lily, I want to give you the best. Baby girl, you're the best thing I never knew I needed and I'll be forever grateful for you."

Maia resumed singing Lily's lullaby, this time changing the lyrics. She sang of every hope she had for her daughter and prayed to God that Lily's life would be better than she herself had ever experienced. Maia didn't know what the future held, but she *did* know that in her twenty-six years of life, the Lord had never failed her and she knew He wouldn't start now.

"I trust You, Lord. I can't see the way, but I trust You."

"Girl, treat yo' self!" Destiny Grant drawled the next day, throwing a box of sugary cereal into Maia's almost-empty shopping cart.

"I don't have *treat yo' self* money, Des," Maia whined, putting the box back on the shelf.

"Consider it my treat," Des replied, throwing it back into the cart. This was Des' usual on their Saturday morning grocery runs.

"I appreciate everything you're doing, Des. I don't know what I'd do without you," Maia said sincerely.

Destiny fanned her hand nonchalantly, waving at nothing in particular.

Maia had met Des at the coffee shop when she first moved to Turnpeake and they'd hit it off like they'd known each other forever. She had ordered a cappuccino and in true Destiny-fashion, struck up a conversation about the origin of the coffee bean which then led to a conversation about soccer and before Maia realized, they'd formed a bond over the most random things.

It didn't take long for Maia to call the dark-skinned beauty her friend. Destiny was the most outspoken, yet honest, selfless, and hilarious person Maia had ever met. She was truly a God-send.

"Maia?" The deep baritone startled Maia from her thoughts. Her eyes darted up to see none other than the bass-playing church boy she'd met last week. As their eyes collided, Maia's cheeks grew hot. Truly this man had been blessed with a double portion when the Lord was doling out looks. Male models would pay for his jawline, not to mention his smile.

"I have died and gone to heaven," Des muttered quietly in her ear. Maia rolled her eyes, responding to Derek's greeting with a less than enthusiastic "hi".

"How are you?" he asked, his characteristic easy-going smile plastered in place. He held a box of cereal in his hand. The blue animated chameleon on the box somehow made the man look less intimidating.

"I'm great, just doing a bit of shopping. How about you?" Maia fiddled with the tiny pink bow at the front of her only maternity blouse. It was an outdated floral number, but it was all she could afford at the moment.

"I'm having a fine Saturdee," Derek replied, tipping an imaginary hat.

Maia tried not to let her eyes stray from his, but it was difficult. Derek really was a looker. His skin looked like he stepped right out of a cocoa butter commercial; dark and smooth. Today he was clad in a pair of old faded cutoffs and another black tee. Maybe black was his "thing".

"Ahem," Des huffed conspicuously, next to Maia. It brought her back to reality.

"Des, this is Derek from Faith Life Temple. Derek, this is my friend, Destiny."

He stepped forward, hand extended for a handshake, and Destiny reciprocated.

"Derek? As in Derek Hunter." Recognition dawned in Des' eyes, her words more of a statement than a question.

Maia noticed that Derek immediately became uncomfortable, his shoulders tightening and smile faltering ever so slightly. He nodded.

"Nice to meet you," he said, instantly turning his attention back to Maia. "I hope Faith Life left a warm impression on you. We'd love to have you both worshipping with us." Derek's eyes flitted to Des' momentarily before landing on Maia again. "That invitation also extends to your family as well. All are welcome," he smiled.

Maia saw understanding dawn in Destiny's eyes and knew instinctively as she saw Des' mouth open, disaster would follow. It was like a horror movie unfolding before her eyes and as much as she wanted to interrupt or distract Destiny, disbelief kept her lips pinned tightly together.

"So, you're interested in my friend," she said matter-of-factly, her eyes meeting his with boldness.

"Destiny!" Maia shrieked, her cheeks growing hot from embarrassment. "I'm so sorry! My friend has no filter between her brain and her mouth!" she said, her voice increasing several decibels with each word. Derek shifted his weight from one foot to the next, looking uncomfortable. His shock seemingly outweighed her own. Maia had never thought about committing murder, but it sure seemed like a viable option right now. "Don't mind her, I know you're just being nice. Thank you for the invitation. I'm sure I'll be visiting Faith Life again sometime."

"Great," Derek smiled, relief causing his furrowed brows to relax. "Alright, well I'll let you get back to your shopping. It was nice seeing you." He turned, abruptly walking back up the aisle.

"I got my eye on you, Mr. Hunter," Des piped up suspiciously, her eyes closing to slits as she squinted at him.

Maia elbowed her hard in the ribs.

"Did you say something?" Derek asked, looking back at them.

"No!" Maia replied quickly before Des could repeat. When he was out of earshot, Maia once again poked her friend in the ribs.

"Ouch!"

"Get used to that because I'm going to kill you," Maia ground out angrily. "Why would you do that?" she shrieked.

"Because it's clear that he likes you," Destiny replied matter-of-factly.

"No, he doesn't! I'm so embarrassed. He was just being nice and you put him in such an awkward position." Maia buried her face in her hands just thinking about how uncomfortable her next meeting with Derek would be.

"You *do* know who that was, right?" Destiny asked.

"He plays the bass at Faith Life. I met him last week."

"He's also Pastor Carl's son, probably thee most sought-after PK bachelor this side of the Mississippi." Destiny shook her head in pity, her look telling Maia this is information she should have known.

"How was I supposed to know? He didn't exactly volunteer that information and he certainly didn't have the air of 'megachurch royalty'. He seems really down to earth."

"Yeah, the whole family is. They're really respected here. Pastor Carl is probably one of the only megachurch pastors in this city who hasn't been in the media for some clandestine affair or mismanaging funds...if you know what I mean. Nevertheless Maia, I know men and he looked at you like you were water in a desert, but I'll drop it," Des conceded.

"I'm five months pregnant with another man's baby, Destiny. I assure you, whatever you picked up from him, was not attraction or interest. He was probably pitying the sad, single mom he met at church."

"There are still good men out there, Maia. You'd do well to remember that every man is not Eli. Anyway, let's pay for these groceries. And I think it goes without saying that we're heading to the house of the Lord tomorrow," Des said cheekily, giving the shopping cart a push and sashaying her ample hips up the aisle.

Maia followed, shaking her head. She'd be heading to church alright, because she needed it. She would also be avoiding Derek Hunter like the plague. Maia didn't need another spoiled church boy in her life, not even as a friend. She'd been taken for a fool once before and she was not going to let it happen again. Ever.

Chapter 4

"So many times in life, we feel like we've messed our lives up beyond repair. I've been there. As many of you know, I was a drug addict and a thief at seventeen. I say that only to encourage you not to lose hope. I wanted nothing to do with God, but He loved me enough to pursue me, even in my rebellion." Derek's voice cracked on the last word and he remained silent for a moment. The congregation sat silent and the anticipation was almost palpable in the auditorium.

"I thought I would never be happy, never be free from addiction, but thanks be to God, I encountered Jesus when I was twenty-one. I was strung out on a street corner, overdosed, and unconscious when I met the Lord. I don't know if it was a dream or if it was real, but I heard the voice of the Lord and I felt His intense love for me. He assured me that my life could be redeemed if I would just choose Him. God spoke clearly of my destiny and how He would use my experiences to help many others. That day, I made a choice that changed my life forever. I woke up in the hospital three days later and things have never been the same. Jesus saved me that day and He can do the same for you today."

Derek continued to speak, but Maia sat in the balcony lost in thought. She was reeling from his candid testimony. He certainly didn't look like what he'd been through. From beside her, Destiny whispered, "Girl, he's a sanctified thug. What more could you want?"

Maia rolled her eyes. "If my baby bump did not clue you in, I'm not looking for a man, least of all a preacher." She'd been totally shell-shocked when he was welcomed to the pulpit as today's speaker.

"Okay. I'm just saying, I'm filled with the Spirit and the Spirit's telling me *this* is going to be a thing."

"Shhh." Maia shushed her friend and turned her attention back to the service. The altar was now flooded with people of all ages as Derek prayed for them. Her heart warmed as she saw the impact of his preaching. People wept and wailed and it was the most beautiful thing she'd ever seen. There was no doubt in her mind that lives were being changed today.

Derek stepped to the mic again. "Before we end the service, I want to let you all know that the Lord can turn any circumstance around for your good. You don't have to finish the way you started. There's a beginning and an end to every story, but the middle is where God does His best work," he finished. Picking up his tablet from the pulpit, he made his way off the stage.

"Come on," Maia nudged Des. "Let's get a move on or it'll take us an hour just to get to the parking lot," she said, rising with the grace of a penguin.

By the time they made it to the exit, Maia's feet ached just a little and she regretted her decision to wear an old, strappy pair of black heels Mimi had bought her. They were impractical to say the least, but she'd wanted to feel beautiful again. There was something about carrying around an extra twenty pounds of weight that made her feel very unattractive most days. They made their way to the aisle and down the steps to the main floor of the church.

"Maia!"

Maia whipped her head around at the sound of her name and the now familiar voice that spoke it. Derek. Her heart drummed loudly in her chest. This couldn't be happening. She refused to develop a crush on another smooth PK. "Hi," she replied, reluctantly turning to face him with a polite smile. "How are you?"

Derek gave a half smile, his lips tilting up to display a cute dimple in his right cheek. She hadn't noticed it before. It made him that much more attractive. Maia shook her head. Here she was getting carried away again. She reminded herself that he was just another man.

"Tired, but good. I'm glad to see you. How are you and baby doing?" he asked casually.

Maia was taken aback by his question. This was the first time he'd acknowledged her baby bump since meeting her. She'd almost begun to think he hadn't noticed she was pregnant. Smiling warmly, her eyes met his. "I'm great. Baby's playing football with my belly button today," Maia replied, her laughter belying the grimace on her face.

Derek chuckled. "Looks like you have an athlete on your hands."

"She's playing offense strong today."

"Haha! Is your-uh-your hus-partner here today?" he asked. His eyes held hers intently despite tripping over his words.

Maia's cheeks flushed. Her heart plummeted, partly because she was embarrassed to be single and partly because of his boldness. Pushing those feelings aside, she held her head high. In the short space of time before she responded, Maia tried to convince herself that she didn't care what he thought. "I don't have a 'hus-partner', it's just me, myself and Lily," she answered, rubbing her baby bump and trying to lighten the awkwardness of the moment.

"Hiiii."

They both turned toward Destiny.

"Whew! That invisibility cloak was heavy," she said, pretending to take off and fold said cloak.

They all chuckled.

"Hi Destiny, how are you?"

"I'm great, Hunter. I'm gonna give you two your privacy. Just know that if you hurt my friend, I'll kill you," she announced, speed walking toward the exit before either of them could protest.

They were left awkwardly staring at each other. Maia bit her lip nervously, suddenly noticing the long queue of people behind Derek, seemingly waiting to speak with him.

"You should probably go," she said, waving her hand in the direction of the line.

"They can wait, Maia." His eyes never left hers. "I-I was wondering, I mean I-I wanted to find out if…" He gave up and began scratching his head. "I'm messing this up royally," Derek grimaced.

"Messing up *what* exactly?" she asked curiously.

"Would you like to go to lunch with me?"

"What?" Shock held Maia's mouth open. She didn't know what she had been expecting, but it certainly wasn't a lunch invitation. Was he asking her on a date?

"Would you like to go to lunch with me? I'd like to get to know you better."

Maia shook her head. "I don't understand. Why?" Her eyes met his boldly, looking for answers to the thousand questions swirling in her head. She found none. Only her own fear of history repeating itself was reflected in his gaze. There was no capacity within her for anymore heartbreak, least of all from another broken preacher's kid. When she left Jacksonville, she had resolved in her heart that she was not going to make the same mistakes. Her heart and body belonged to the Lord now.

"The truth is, I find you intriguing, Maia. There's something about your spirit that makes me want to learn more about you. I saw you praying on the floor when you thought no one was watching and I'd like to learn more about you."

Her heart did a funny dance for the first time since meeting this man and Maia couldn't figure out if he was blind or just plain crazy. She was not unaware of the optics of her predicament. Few men, least of all a preacher, would be willing to put themselves in this position, but yet here was this unicorn of a man, putting it all on the line in public. Despite his boldness, she prepared herself to decline.

"I'm sorry, I can't. I appreciate you asking, but I'm not looking for any new friends, acquaintances, or anything else for that matter. It's just me and Jesus for now. Thank you for asking though." Maia smiled self-consciously, painfully aware of the line of people waiting to speak to Derek. She cast a glance behind him at the line and stares of speculation greeted her.

"Okay. I understand. If you change your mind, the invitation still stands."

"I'll keep that in mind. I should get going. Enjoy the rest of your day."

Maia turned and briskly walked toward Destiny, her heart beating loudly in her ears.

"Let's go, Des."

They walked outside and Maia wished she could leave behind all thoughts of Derek Hunter as easily as she left the compound of that church.

Chapter 5

Destiny commandeered Maia's kitchen after church, insisting that she could handle the cooking. After demolishing the scrumptious chicken casserole Des made, the two women sat chatting comfortably.

"Give me one good reason why you won't give *preacher-boy* a chance to sweep you off your feet? I have an eye for bs and I don't see any in him, girl. At least give him a chance," Des said.

Maia threw a foot over the armrest of her leather one-seater, shooting a glance at her friend who sat at her tiny dining table painting her fingernails *deep dark red*.

"Well, for starters, I'm pregnant. Forgive me for being a little skeptical of a guy who's so eager to pursue a woman who's pregnant with another man's child. After what happened with Eli—"

"I know that was difficult and traumatic. I'd punch that coward in the nuts if I ever met him, but sweetie, you can't charge a good man in your present season for the sins of a lesser man from your past. You deserve happiness just as much as the next woman and I think you should give Hunter a chance."

Maia didn't respond immediately. Des' words hung heavily in the air. She felt that oh so familiar check in her heart and knew it was Lord. She still wasn't convinced enough to accept Derek's invitation to lunch. However, she was at least willing to admit that there *was* a crippling fear that gripped her every time she thought about opening her heart up to another man.

She couldn't continue like this. Something had to give. Closing her eyes, she said a silent prayer to the Lord for healing and restoration. Maia looked forward to the day when her heart would be unencumbered by the past, a day when she would be able to love freely again.

"I hear you, Des. I do. I guess I just need some time. Even *you* have to admit that there's something strange about this man being interested in a pregnant single mom. There are a gazillion women in that church he could ask on a date. Why me?"

"Why *not* you, honey?" Des raised an eyebrow as she blew on her painted fingernails. "You are a beautiful, intelligent, kind, woman of faith. You made one mistake and even God has worked *that* for your good. I know you love Lily with all of your being already. I guess...I'm just asking you not to give up on love."

Not willing to concede, Maia released a noncommittal grunt. "I talked to Sarah and it looks like I'll be able to get paid maternity leave," she revealed, shamelessly changing the subject.

Des looked up, clearly aware of the redirection. She harrumphed, but went along with the change in topic. "That's great! One less thing to worry about. God got you girl."

"Yeah, God got me," Maia replied, smiling.

"People are talking, D. You don't have the luxury of lounging with a pregnant woman in the halls of the church without gossip following. Your mother and I are worried about you." Carl Hunter's face was laced with worry as he said the words.

As if on cue, Coretta Hunter piped up, "What's going on, baby? This isn't like you. We haven't even seen you talk to a woman since that Johnson girl did what she did. Why are you so intent on pursuing this woman? Going this road will be complicated at best and catastrophic at worst. What do we really know about her besides the fact that she's pregnant out of wedlock? Is she even a Christian?"

Derek pursed his lips. This onslaught was *not* what he expected when he came over for Sunday dinner with his parents, but he should have known this was coming. He glanced across the oval, wooden dining table at his parents' worried faces.

"Mama, I didn't come here for an interrogation. I'm not 'pursuing' anyone. I've seen Maia all of three times, but I hear you and I'll be more circumspect in the future." The finality in his voice was enough for his parents and they visibly relaxed, their shoulders dropping ever so slightly.

"Your daddy and I trust your judgment. We aren't telling you *not* to date her. We're just telling you to be careful. That being said, we're not going to beat a dead horse. You're an adult."

Derek was pretty sure this conversation would not be the end of the matter, but at least his parents were satisfied with his explanation. Truth be told, they'd made some valid points. He'd known the gossip mill would be abuzz the moment he stopped Maia at church. And while he was not afraid of the gossip, he didn't want Maia being scathed by their cruelty.

His parents were right, he needed to put an end to his efforts to get to know Maia. Derek refused to go down such a life-altering path so recklessly, with nothing but intuition guiding him. If it was the Lord's will that they be connected, He'd have to do it Himself.

Derek hungrily dug into the baked mac and cheese on his plate, determined to forget about the entire situation and even more determined to leave Maia alone. She clearly wasn't interested in getting to know him anyway.

Chapter 6

As the weeks went by, Maia marveled at the Lord's faithfulness. She could now think of her grandmother and Eli without bitterness taking over. Forgiving them, though difficult, gave her a freedom she couldn't quite explain. She only knew that it felt like someone had lifted a gigantic boulder off her shoulders. Despite her belly now being the size of a large watermelon, Maia felt free. Work was becoming ever-increasingly difficult, but she didn't want to start maternity leave until Lily was here. She wanted as much time with her daughter as possible before going back to work.

It was after midnight, but sleep escaped her; partially because Lily was attempting to do somersaults in her tummy and partially because her dinner still sat heavily in her stomach despite the fact that she ate it hours ago. The sauce and cheese from the lasagna were responsible for her current discomfort.

Lying in bed, she reflected on the past three weeks of her life. As they sometimes did, her thoughts drifted to Derek. Since she had turned down his date invitation, he completely backed off. Each Sunday at church, she was now greeted from a distance with a polite nod or a smile.

Maia wondered if he'd heard the swirling gossip as well. She had overheard two middle-aged women talking about her in one of the church's restrooms. They hadn't known she was in one of the stalls and had called her everything but a child of God, insinuating that she was trying to snag the pastor's son for money and influence. Allowing her pettiness to get the better of her, Maia had sauntered out of the stall with a wide smile and polite greeting. She chuckled as she recalled the horrified looks on their faces. The gossip hadn't surprised her… She had "been there and done that" in Jacksonville. Maia just hoped Derek wouldn't be crucified by the church mafia for their one conversation in the church lobby.

Her mind drifted to her conversation with Destiny. Maybe her friend was right. Perhaps Maia's reservations about him were based solely on her insecurities. After all, he had done nothing to make her question his motives. Her last relationship had been a disaster and she feared that every subsequent relationship would be colored by her experience with Eli. She prayed that it wouldn't be so. If Des was right about Derek being a good match (and that was big **if**), the Lord would have to make it undeniably obvious.

Silencing her loud thoughts was not easy, but she eventually drifted off to sleep, dreaming of wedding dresses and sunflowers. Unbeknownst to her, they told the story of her future, one she didn't yet have eyes to see.

Derek sat on his favorite park bench and watched as the sun set over downtown Turnpeake. Periodically, the sun was obstructed by some imposing skyscraper, casting a shadow over the park. There were a few people jogging and a family of five still soaking in what little light was left. The couple sat on a bench on the far side of the park as three curly-haired boys played messily in a small sandbox. Derek had been sitting here for the last hour and witnessed at least five fights among the tiny humans. The parents were oblivious.

Despite being at a random park in the middle of the city, they looked at home with each other. The petite Asian woman sat comfortably, her head resting in the crook of the man's arm. He could be a linebacker for how huge he was; his dark skin contrasted her much paler complexion, but they somehow did not look out of place. They sat in silence, but their faces spoke volumes. Contentment like that couldn't be faked.

Suddenly the woman tilted her head up, looking at her partner. He smiled at her and lowered his head to kiss her. Derek immediately looked away, feeling like an irreverent third party in someone else's thoughts. He turned his eyes toward the fading sun, wishing it was just as easy to turn his heart away from wanting a love that felt like home.

He had no explanation for the sudden change in his thinking or desires. For the last six years, simply doing the Lord's work had filled him with contentment. Derek spent most of his time at his non-profit, mentoring the young men under his charge, playing basketball with them, and trying to be the best example of a man he could be. He and his team didn't always get it right, but they always showed up, and sometimes that's all the boys needed.

It wasn't that he didn't want marriage and a family, it just hadn't been a priority. Truth be told, he had become exhausted with the forward women who threw themselves at him. He was often propositioned for sex by women who would be letting "hallelujahs" rain the following Sunday in church. The dating pool was far too treacherous and after what happened with Jessica, he just hadn't been able to put his heart in the hands of another woman. The pain and public humiliation he'd endured had left an indelible mark on his life and since then, the risk that came with loving a woman always seemed too great. Derek shifted uncomfortably in his seat as unwanted memories of his past flooded his mind. He was immediately catapulted to the moment his world came crashing down…

Chapter 7

Turnpeake, Texas

13 years ago

"You're what?" Derek heard the words coming out of his mouth, but somehow it seemed like someone else was saying them. The room felt like it was spinning. "How can you be pregnant, Jess? We've never even…"

"I'm sorry, D."

Jess' eyes refused to meet his. Instead, her fingers twirled the tight coils of her kinky hair. Derek felt an unfamiliar emotion unfurl in his chest as he came to grips with what she was saying. It was pure unadulterated rage. He wanted to shout and throw things and destroy everything in her room that dared to stay the same when his heart was crumbling. Clenching his fists tightly, Derek dug his nails into his palms until the physical pain drowned out his desire to tear her room apart.

"Whose is it?" he asked, forcing the words through clenched teeth.

"It doesn't matter. He doesn't want anything to do with me or the baby," she replied, tears welling in her brown eyes and spilling onto her cheeks.

For the first time since they'd met in elementary school, her waterworks did not soften his heart. In fact, as he began to put the puzzle pieces together, he knew he had to leave before this anger consumed him.

"Is that why you've been trying so hard to get me to have sex with you? You wanted someone to pin this on?" Derek recalled her relentless attempts to seduce him over the past few weeks.

She began crying in earnest now, a river of tears flowing down her cheeks. Derek couldn't care less at the moment. He rose from her bed, knowing he'd never sit there again. This had been his second home for almost a decade and now he couldn't even bear to look at the pink patterned wallpaper he'd teased Jess about since the moment she got it. He steeled himself to walk away from the girl he thought he'd marry.

"Please don't go. I'm sorry," Jess said, barely able to get the words out as the sobs wracked her body.

"I never want to see you again," Derek ground out, leaving without a second glance. As he walked down the stairs of her house, he felt the weight of everything hit him all at once. The anger fell away like a broken shell, leaving him with nothing but raw pain. He tried to stop the tears from falling, but it was useless. He wiped them aggressively from his face as he descended the steps and hurried toward the front door.

"Are you leaving already, D? I thought you were staying for dinner, dear," Mrs. Johnson's airy voice drifted from the kitchen.

Derek did not look across the hall to the kitchen. He couldn't. His world felt like it was crumbling and the last thing he needed was an audience.

"No, Mrs. Johnson. I have to go."

His voice was hoarse from the tears and sounded foreign even to him. He didn't give her a chance to ask any more questions. Pushing the front door, he ran out and didn't stop running until he was home.

"I never want to see you again…"

Those were the last words he said to Jessica Johnson, but it wasn't the last time he'd seen her. She and her parents had continued to attend Faith Life Temple until Jess' pregnancy became impossible to conceal. Then the gossip had started and while Jess had been honest with him, she hadn't been as forthcoming with her parents or the rest of the church for that matter. She had told everyone the baby was his and the tale had spread like wildfire among the congregation.

Luckily his parents had believed him and after a very tense meeting with Jess' parents, she finally broke down and told the truth. That did nothing to quell the gossip and slander though. After the Johnsons realized the gossip was becoming too much for Jess, they not only left the church, but left Texas altogether. Derek never saw her again, and honestly he was happy they left. Her lie had been like a scarlet letter on his forehead and even though it took some time for the rumors to dissipate after they left, eventually the truth won out like it always does. True to fashion, the church paparazzi sourced pictures of the baby and it was obvious Derek had no genetic ties to the mixed-race newborn Jessica had held in her arms.

Just thinking about those times brought back the memory of his turmoil and frustration. He whispered a quiet "thank You" to the Lord for bringing him through all of it. Even though he had wanted nothing to do with God back then, he could see the Lord's faithfulness in hindsight. That entire ordeal was the cause of his spiral into a life of violence and addiction. He had vowed never to let love make a fool out of him again and he'd stood by his word thus far.

He dated and had meaningless sex with women after Jess, but he had never gotten close to opening up to another woman again. After he dedicated his life to the Lord, Derek had metaphorically locked his heart and thrown away the key. That's why his reaction and behavior toward Maia was shocking, even to himself. He shifted uncomfortably on the park bench. How had she made it into his thoughts...again?

After his parents' intervention, he completely shut down the possibility of any kind of relationship with Maia, even a platonic one. She often drifted into his thoughts unwelcomed though, to the point that he prayed for God to help him let it go. His heart was constantly at war with his mind about the inexplicable draw he felt towards her. He knew that any way the dice landed, she was coming with baggage and he wasn't talking about the innocent child she was carrying. She had a past he knew nothing about and he knew he had to stop entertaining thoughts about her if he wanted to move on. Since she'd turned him down, he'd been perfectly polite and distant, and he fully intended on continuing in that way. He'd left all his cards on the table and if they were to become anything more, the next move had to be hers.

Derek felt certifiable every time his thoughts landed on *her*. Never in his wildest imagination did he think that he could be this captivated by someone who was about to have a child that was not his. But somewhere inside of him, past his fear of the unknown, was a certainty that he was on the right path.

He recalled the prayer he'd spoken in his heart after he realized there would be no forgetting Maia Miller… "Lord, if she's the one, let her change her mind about the date." He wasn't holding his breath, though. At this point in his life, he wanted God's will; nothing more, nothing less, and nothing else.

Chapter 8

As another Monday morning dawned hot and clear, Maia looked around the busy corner cafe where she worked. She just knew this day was going to be a doozy. It was barely 8am and every table was occupied. The morning coffee rush was finally dwindling and Maia felt like she could breathe again. After fulfilling the remaining orders, she plopped unceremoniously onto a chair behind the counter, praying for just five minutes of reprieve from incoming traffic.

Pulling the phone from her pocket, she shot a quick reply to a text from Des. Just then, she heard the metallic clink of the cafe door opening. A heavy sigh escaped her lips. So much for a break. Shoving the phone back into her pocket, Maia mentally prepared herself for the ankle ache that assailed her each time she stood. Although she usually took pride in being present, today she was tired…

Rising to her feet without looking up, she rattled off her rehearsed greeting and waited for the order.

"Hey there, Maia."

Her head whipped up at the familiar baritone.

"Derek! H-hi." She tried telling herself that her racing heart was the result of being startled, but she was beginning to think that maybe his smile had something to do with it. Seriously, the man could easily do a Colgate commercial. His smile was perfect, especially now, when it caused his eyes to crinkle at the corners and his pupils to glitter, despite their dark hue. She silently admonished herself for losing herself in his eyes again. He was little more than a stranger for crying out loud.

"I didn't know you worked here. What are the odds? I work across the street, but I'm not much of a caffeine drinker so I've never ventured inside."

"Well, what brings you in today?" Maia asked curiously

"I wanted to do something nice for my team at work. We're having a meeting this morning and I thought donuts would be a great start to the day."

"That's sweet."

"How are you? How's Lily doing?" he asked, leaning over and resting his forearms on the dark chrome countertop.

"Um— Lily and I are doing well. Thanks for asking," she replied, noting that he actually remembered Lily's name. "How are you, Derek?"

"I'm good, a lot better now that I've seen you," he said with a smile.

Maia's eyes narrowed. She couldn't tell from his tone whether he was flirting or just being nice.

"What kind of donuts would you like?" she returned, ignoring his previous statement. Truthfully, she wasn't sure how to respond to it.

"Uh— I'll take two of each flavor."

"Sure." She nodded and set about packaging the donuts. After ringing up his order, she slid the two large boxes across the counter.

"Thank you, Maia. Have a wonderful day." Derek flashed her a smile and turned to leave. A second later he swiveled to look at her again. "I know this is gonna seem weird," he started, resting the donuts on the counter, and reaching for the wallet in his back pocket, "and I want you to know there are absolutely no strings attached to this. I won a voucher for a massage in a community center raffle about a month ago, but massages aren't really my thing. It just occurred to me to give it to you."

Derek unfolded the voucher and scanned the paper briefly. "Yes, pregnancy massages are included. I'm sure it's tough being on your feet all day. It's yours...if you want," he continued, holding a letter sized piece of paper out to her.

"Um...thank you, Derek, but I can't accept this," she answered softly. In spite of her refusal, Maia looked longingly at the voucher. Even with his assurance that there were no conditions attached, pride would not allow her to accept his offer.

"Are you sure? You'd be doing me a favor taking it off my hands," he persuaded.

Maia hesitated. A massage certainly sounded like heaven and his offer *was* incredibly thoughtful. Folding her arms and looking at him pensively, she responded with a question of her own. "What made you decide to give me the voucher in the first place?"

Derek shifted his weight from one foot to the other, before looking at his shoes or perhaps, the ground. Maia couldn't be sure.

"Honestly, I was about to leave and it just popped into my mind. I can't explain why, but I felt like I *needed* to give it to you." With his head still hung, Derek shot her an apprehensive glance from under his lashes, as if expecting her to drag him off for psychological evaluation.

Maia nodded in acknowledgment, willing his eyes to meet hers again. After a moment of silence, he finally lifted his head.

"Okay, Derek, I accept. Thank you for your kindness. You have no idea how much I appreciate it."

His eyes widened at her words, before he grinned and wiped his brow in relief. "Whew! So, you don't think I'm a bit loony?" he asked humorously, handing over the voucher.

"Well, the jury's still out on *that*," Maia teased.

Derek released a burst of deep, hearty laughter and she joined him.

"I appreciate your honesty, Ms. Miller," he replied, through his chuckles.

"Seriously, this was extremely thoughtful of you, Derek. Thank you."

"Don't worry about it," he countered, waving her appreciation away. "I'll get out of your hair now. See you around, Maia." Picking up the donuts, he turned to leave again.

"Derek..." Maia called, even though she wasn't sure what would come out of her mouth next.

He turned around again, eyebrows raised.

"Is that offer for lunch still on the table?"

"Yes, yes, it is."

"I'd like to take you up on that— as friends."

"Of course. There's no pressure here," Derek smiled.

His eyes crinkled at the corners and twinkled. She'd never met anyone with eyes like black diamonds before. Maia didn't want to admit it, but his smile changed the rhythm of her heart. It never failed to bemuse her.

They arranged a Saturday lunch date, exchanged phone numbers and then he left, crossing the street to the center for young men. Maia released a shaky breath, hoping to God she wasn't making a mistake. She dialed the number for the spa and made an appointment. A massage was exactly what she needed.

Dinner that evening consisted of boxed macaroni and cheese and iced tea. It wasn't what Maia wanted, but it was what she could afford. After she paid her insurance and rent, there was little left for anything else and she didn't want to max out her credit card on food when she needed so many other things for Lily's arrival.

After quitting her corporate entry level job over five months ago, Maia had packed up her entire life; which consisted of two suitcases of clothes, her rocking chair, and a beat-up guitar. Mimi had gifted her the instrument when she was twelve and she'd taught herself how to play. The comfort it brought made Turnpeake feel a little more like home.

Moving to a new city was not for the faint of heart, but moving to a new city while pregnant was certifiably insane. It was a leap of faith like none she'd taken before. Some would say it was just plain stupid, but after Mimi had kicked her out, Maia had felt so alone and devastated, she'd needed a fresh start. After resigning with immediate effect, she'd packed up Ginger with everything she owned and started driving. Maia hadn't known where she was headed at the time, but she knew she needed to escape Eli's lies and the shame she felt every time Mimi looked at her.

She'd thought her worst day would forever be when she realized that her mother wasn't coming back for her, but the look on Mimi's face after she revealed her pregnancy, had broken Maia's heart. As a deaconess in the church, her grandmother had worshipped the very ground that the pastor walked on and she refused to believe Maia when she revealed that his son was the baby's father. Could she really blame her though? Eli had sworn on everything but the name of the Lord that he hadn't touched her. His denial had broken her heart in a way she couldn't even comprehend.

Maia expected him to eventually confess, but no such thing happened. His cowardice had been constant 'til the day she left Jacksonville. And now here she was, months later, no longer angry, but still disappointed that Lily wouldn't know the love of her father.

Chapter 9

Derek stood outside of Apartment 21 in the rundown city complex. He was extremely nervous and didn't know why. It was just lunch after all. Yet still, a trickle of sweat ran down his forehead and he swiftly wiped it away. He tugged the front of his blue polo a few times to generate some cool air, then knocked on the door.

"Coming!"

He heard Maia's musical voice in the distance and smiled. This was really happening, he thought to himself just before the door opened. Maia stood, looking up at him with a smile. The white floral summer dress she wore complimented her honey-colored skin to perfection and her natural curls framed her face perfectly. She looked youthful and undeniably beautiful.

"Hi. These are for you." He pulled the bouquet of freshly cut sunflowers from behind his back and presented them to her. "They match your dress," Derek continued awkwardly. Why were his hands sweating? He'd not been this nervous in years and he had no idea what it was about this woman that brought out the boy in him, but it was disconcerting to say the least.

Maia looked down at herself, then back up at him in surprise. "Look at that...they do. These are my favorite flowers, you know. Thank you, Derek," Maia said with a warm smile. "I'll just go put these in some water and I'll be right back." She disappeared again, leaving the door slightly ajar. Derek took another deep breath and tried to pull himself together. This was just a friendly lunch for crying out loud. There was no reason for his stomach to be doing somersaults.

When Maia returned, they left for the restaurant, chatting easily about her adjustment to a new city. Derek couldn't help but notice that his anxiety dissipated as they talked more and more. Maybe they *would* have a great time after all.

As they talked over lunch, Derek marveled at the ease with which the conversation flowed. He soon learned that Maia was quick-witted with a dry sense of humor that had them both cracking up throughout their meal. Even now, as they sat at an outdoor table at the small cafe where they'd eaten, there was a deep peace he felt in her presence. It made no sense to his natural mind. Their conversation was light, but this peace spoke volumes. Even though they'd both finished their meal, they sat talking comfortably, neither of them eager to leave.

"If you could spend your life doing anything in the world - no restrictions - what would you do?" he asked curiously, resting his elbows on the tiny wooden table and leaning into the conversation.

"I'd become a bird, something formidable...like an eagle. Flying *and* being scary? Priceless," she replied, animatedly.

Derek chuckled. Her words sounded serious, but humor made her eyes twinkle as she said them.

"Seriously speaking, if I had no restrictions and unlimited resources, I'd help people, single moms and children especially. I'd build shelters and help people get on their feet again. I've always dreamed of…like…creating a haven of sorts for battered women and mothers, helping them heal and grow, equipping them to provide for their children and themselves. Before I moved here, I volunteered at a women's shelter on weekends and it was so fulfilling to see the restoration and redemption that took place. I'm sorry for babbling on. That's probably not what you were expecting." She pulled nervously on one of her curls, stretching it until it escaped her fingers and recoiled into her twist out.

Derek caught her eye and held her gaze captive with his. "Maia, if there's one thing you'll never have to do in my presence, it's minimize the things you're passionate about. I find your enthusiasm quite captivating."

Her skin flushed red and she ducked her head, trying to disappear in her mane of dark curls. "Thank you. That means a lot," she smiled shyly, peeking from behind her twist out.

Maia's soft brown eyes hit him like a bus in that moment and he felt the impact deep in his chest. He didn't like the way his heart twisted as she looked across the table at him. The feelings her gaze evoked were foreign to him and there were no words he could use to adequately describe them. He averted his eyes, aware that she probably thought his staring was weird to say the least.

Clearing his throat, Derek added, "I-I'm amazed at your passion. Many people have noble aspirations, but seldom put action to those desires. I think it's incredible that you gave of your time and energy to help others."

"Enough about me," Maia replied, blushing. "What wakes you up in the morning, Mr. Hunter?"

"I think I'm as passionate about seeing young men's lives transformed as you are about women and children. I run The Pidyon Center opposite the coffee shop. Essentially, we mentor boys, help rehabilitate young men who've done time, or those who have an addiction, and try our best to ensure that they don't return to the streets. There's a lot more involved, but that's the condensed version," Derek chuckled.

Maia's eyes widened and her lips parted slowly. "Wow. So, how did you start working there?"

"Um— I'm the founder. After what I went through, I don't think I had a choice. Helping men like myself who couldn't seem to climb out of the pits of addiction became the only option for me. If Jesus could turn *my* life around, He can do the same and even more for the men and boys that I talk to everyday. That's how we change the world: one person at a time, one city at a time. I was the one lost sheep that Jesus came after and I wanted to do the same for others, to be a consistent voice of truth and encouragement to men, in a world that often discards them because of their past. I worked on a plan, rounded up a few trustworthy friends and worked hard to get funding. The rest is history."

"I'm honestly blown away, Derek. You certainly are an anomaly. I don't even understand why I feel the need to say this. It doesn't make any sense because we don't know each other that well, but I'm proud of you. I sense the Lord is too," Maia responded.

His stomach tightened at her words. Why did they affect him so deeply? He was beginning to think that it was something he'd just have to accept instead of trying to understand. Their eyes met and stayed locked for half a minute too long. It left Derek feeling bare, like his entire soul was put on display for the woman sitting across from him.

Just then, the waiter came with the bill, unapologetically interrupting the moment. Derek settled it and they got up to leave. He found himself searching his mind for any reason for this date not to end. Date? He silently admonished himself. This was just lunch, nothing more.

As they walked away from their table, the words left his mouth before he could recall them, "Would you like to go get some ice-cream?"

"I'd love to," Maia answered quickly.

They strode to his Camaro which he'd parallel parked in front of the cafe and climbed in. Derek started it up and the engine hummed as heavily as his heart did at that moment. Three words were stuck in his throat, trying to fight their way out of his mouth. It was a fight he was losing.

"I like you." Even with the engine running, his words sounded like a sonic boom in the small interior of the car.

"I like you too, Derek," Maia responded. "I had a great time today." The levity in her tone was unmistakable.

"No, Maia," he said, catching her eyes with his and holding them captive. "I like you, like you."

Chapter 10

Destiny's screech echoed loudly from Maia's small bathroom. A few seconds later, she came marching into the living room where Maia sat, a look of disbelief on her face.

A burst of laughter left Maia's lips. Half of Des' hair hung in bouncy twists on her shoulders while the other half defied gravity in the biggest afro Maia had ever seen. She looked comical with her mouth hanging open in shock.

"Well, come on! Don't keep me waiting! What did you say?" Des exclaimed. She frantically waved her rat-tailed comb in the air as if it would make Maia answer faster.

"I told him I liked him too," Maia mumbled the words, avoiding Des' gaze.

Destiny stood with her lips parted in an exaggerated "o" until Maia was genuinely concerned.

"You know, it's not totally out of the realm of possibility that I'd tell the truth," she quipped.

"I'm proud of you, sis, for giving love another chance. So…what now?"

"We've been texting and talking on the phone all week. We're keeping it light. I don't want to be hurt again and I know this isn't exactly a conventional situation. I'm not expecting anything given the fact that I'm about to give birth in a few months," Maia replied, somehow managing to sound excited and dejected at the same time.

"Uh-uh! You don't get to do this. You don't get to disqualify yourself from happiness because you've made mistakes. You are not damaged goods. Actually, your past makes you a prime candidate for redemption, Maia. Just let go and enjoy the journey."

As Des' words reached her ears, Maia could tell that they came straight from the heart of God. In that moment, she could think of a million different reasons why she didn't deserve to be happy, but all of those reasons crumbled as Des' words washed over her and hope, though faint and microscopic, bloomed in her heart. Maybe just maybe...

"Thank you, friend. I needed those words," Maia said warmly. "I appreciate all of the ways you've supported me when I didn't feel like I could stand anymore. You've been so helpful and present these last few months. I wish I could do more for you."

Destiny rarely got emotional. Though animated and extroverted, she was always composed, but in this moment, her eyes softened. "You've done more than you know, Maia. Growing up in foster care, I was told countless times that I'd never amount to anything. My last foster parents told me I'd never make it as an artist so I became a lawyer instead. When I finally got the courage to pick back up my brushes again, I had no idea how I'd promote or get my pieces sold. Then you appeared with nothing but encouragement, grit, and tenacity to spare. You not only showed up at every one of my exhibits, but you handed out flyers at the cafe when you'd only known me for a month. You were my personal cheerleader and I'll forever be grateful. You supported my dream Maia, and I'll never forget that."

"Awwwww, look at you, being all mushy. That's what friends are for, hun," Maia teased.

Destiny rolled her eyes. "And that's all the mush you'll be getting out of me for the rest of the year," she said with a chuckle, returning to the bathroom after giving her rat-tailed comb a sassy twirl in the air.

Maia remained on the couch mulling over her date with Derek. A week had passed since their date and while she'd just admitted her feelings to Destiny, she still had not come to grips with them herself. She enjoyed every conversation with Derek. He called her more than he texted which she appreciated immensely. And they laughed so much, her cheeks hurt after every call. But she didn't want to expect too much from their relationship. Knowing that she could not endure another heartbreak, made each step she took with Derek a tentative one.

After receiving her massage earlier, Maia felt like a new woman. Her body was relaxed and felt more limber than it had in weeks. Her ankles were their normal size again, she was genuinely happy for the first time in many months and a certain dark-skinned guitar player was a large part of that happiness. Derek was hilarious, witty, and kind. Even though they'd only been consistently talking for one week, she felt an undeniable connection to him that was not based on anything tangible. There was some immaterial quality that existed in the way he spoke and responded to her that made Maia feel understood. When she talked, he truly listened and that was something she'd never experienced. He never shied away from the topic of her pregnancy, but he also didn't push for more information than she volunteered. His patience made her feel safe to go at her own pace. It was refreshing.

Just then, her phone rang. She looked at the screen to see Derek's name flashing in green. Her heart immediately fluttered as it always did. She picked up. "Hey."

"Hello Mai. How are you?" he asked cheerily.

Maia blushed. Derek was the only person who'd ever shortened her name. She teased him the first time he'd used it, but now it was growing on her. "I'm great, had my massage today and I feel like me again. How about you?"

"I'm fantastic. I'm about to make a grocery run and then I have a basketball game at Pidyon later. By the way, you have an open invitation to come visit. I'm there most Saturdays, so if you're ever up for it, just let me know and we can arrange."

"You play ball?" she asked incredulously, completely skipping over everything else he said.

"Why do you sound so surprised?" Derek asked. "Do you watch?"

"Do I watch?" Maia scoffed. "Mr. Hunter, you're talking to Rizota High's most famous point guard to date. We were three-time state championship winners. Heck, my name is still on the wall at Rizota." She smiled as her words brought back a flood of high school memories. Maia waited for a response, but there was nothing but silence on the other end. "Derek, are you there?"

"Yes," he replied startled. "Y-you like basketball?" His voice filled with awe.

"It's not that shocking. Women play basketball too."

"I know...I've just never met any as cool as you," he answered, still sounding like she said unicorns were real.

"Uhhh— thanks, I think," Maia chuckled. "I'm feeling pretty great today. I can go with you to the Center later if you'd like."

"Sure. Sounds great. Would you like me to take you?"

He'd never say it, but she saw the way he looked at Ginger. He thought her truck was a death trap. She giggled.

"You know, Ginger is not as bad as you think. She's still got a few miles left in her."

She could hear his smile through the phone.

"I hope you don't take this the wrong way, but Ginger needs to be euthanized. She's on life support at this point," Derek said dryly.

Maia couldn't hold back the sputtering laughter that left her lips. "I won't have you speaking about my truck like that." She tried to put as much sternness in her voice as possible, but her laughter was unconvincing.

"So, I'll pick you up at five. How does that sound?"

"Great, I'll be ready. Hope you're ready to play your butt off or I'll be roasting you the whole way home."

He cackled. "We'll see, won't we?"

"That we shall. I'll see you in a few, Derek."

Maia hung up to catch Destiny unashamedly eavesdropping from the bathroom.

"Well, it looks like we both have dates today," Des said, grinning broadly.

They'd talked at length earlier about Destiny's imminent entry into the world of blind dating. A coworker at Des' law firm insisted that she had the perfect guy for her and after months of horrific dates with other men, Destiny had finally agreed. After all, what could it hurt? He couldn't be worse than the ones her friend had encountered in the online dating pool over the past few months. From drug dealers to secretly married men, she had seen it all. Maia hoped for the best, for her friend's sake.

"It looks that way. Look at us doing our thing, girl," Maia replied sassily, rising to go get ready.

"Got that right," Destiny quipped. "I'll just finish up my hair and then head home to get dressed. I hope to God that Reagan hasn't set me up with a dud."

"Keep an open mind, Destiny!" Maia chided, as she disappeared into her room.

"My mind *is* open. Not my fault my dating life is the epitome of Murphy's Law," Des muttered in response.

"There's only one place to go from there and that's up, my friend."

Chapter 11

One thing was for sure and two for certain, Derek Hunter was fit and he could play some basketball. Maia watched the game on the edge of her seat. He surprised her. It was almost half-time and he'd scored the majority of the points for his team. Each team comprised of both mentors and mentees and their pregame huddles consisted of prayer and overly confident banter. She couldn't help but notice how the teenage boys looked up to Derek and the other mentors; from their special handshakes, to affectionate pats on the back, their bond was undeniable.

They held the game in an indoor court located in the middle of the Pidyon complex, which was much bigger than it looked from the outside. Seats extended on either side of the court and both sides were packed with people, presumably parents and friends of the boys. Derek introduced her to some of the wives of the other mentors and they sat together to watch the men.

Maia couldn't remember any of the names of the almost fifteen women she was introduced to. She now sat to the left of one of them who had spent the entire first half talking about her husband's ten properties across the world, her designer bag collection, and how much money they were going to make by year end. After half an hour of her incessant chatter, Maia was exhausted. All she wanted to do was watch the game, but the leggy blonde made it impossible to focus.

Not for the first time, Maia looked to the quiet brunette to her left for rescue. It was the second time Chatty Cathy had lulled in conversation and Maia was not about to miss her way of escape. For the first time, the beautiful woman, who looked to be of Asian descent, happened to be looking in her direction. Maia pleaded with her eyes for a way of escape. Derek had introduced them, but her name eluded Maia at the moment. Lisa….Laura? It was something with an "L".

"Do you come to these games often?" Maia asked quickly.

The woman smiled and Maia noted that she was even more stunning when she did so.

"They do them once a month and I'm always here. Hubby loves the support," she smiled shyly.

"Aww, that's sweet. Which one's your husband?" Maia queried, scanning the court.

"The one in the blue shoes," the woman replied, pointing to a curly haired blond guy currently running with the ball. Derek had introduced him, but this man's name was also lost in the myriad of names he called.

Nodding in response, Maia decided to go with honesty. "I'm sorry, Derek introduced me to so many people. Can you remind me of your name?" Maia looked sufficiently embarrassed and the woman laughed airily in response.

"That's ok, darling. I'm Lian. You're Maia, right?"

For the first time, Maia heard the faint trace of an English accent.

"Yeah. It's nice to meet you, Lian."

"Katie can be a bit much," Lian whispered sympathetically, her eyes darting to Chatty Cathy who was now assailing the man sitting on the other side of her. She was too busy gushing about her husband's interest in purchasing a private jet to notice them.

Maia chuckled, pursing her lips to avoid commenting on her encounter with Katie. "So, how did your husband end up being a mentor?"

"James and Derek are best friends. Shortly after Derek started the Center, James got on board. Derek runs the admin ship and James and his team recruit new donors and handle the finances. It's a wonder they still find time to mentor, really."

Just then the half-time whistle blared and the teams rushed to the sidelines. Before she could respond to Lian, both Derek and James ran up the bleachers to where they sat.

"I see you ladies are getting on," James noted. His English accent was much thicker than Lian's and now that he was up close, Maia noticed he had two full sleeves of tattoos. He looked like a heartbreaker and Maia couldn't help but wonder how this muscular, sandy-haired *bad boy* had ended up with the petite and soft-spoken Lian.

"Yeah, I quite like Maia, love," Lian revealed, smiling at Maia before turning soft eyes toward her husband. Her eyes drifted over James, starting from his toes until their eyes met. The way she looked at him was almost inappropriate. Maia blushed and so did James. His skin, which was flushed from playing, somehow got redder and he leaned to give his wife a peck on the lips.

"The game will be over soon," James whispered.

"Oh, get a room, you two," Derek teased, sharing a conspiratorial glance with Maia.

James guffawed.

"Don't be jealous, mate," he scoffed, giving him a slight tap on the back before heading to the court.

Derek stayed behind, turning his attention to Maia. "Are you comfortable? Do you need anything?"

"I'm great. Looks like you were being modest, LeBron. That crossover was mean," Maia answered with sparkling eyes.

He chuckled and popped an imaginary collar. "You know, I've got a few tricks up my sleeve."

Maia laughed. "Okay, show off."

Lian cleared her throat. "Not to interrupt your banter, but I think they need you for the game, D."

Derek's team stood by the sidelines, all looking at him askance.

"Yeah. I should get back. I'll see you two after the game."

Lian turned curious eyes on her as Derek ran back to the court and with the most boldness Maia had seen from her so far, she said, "He likes you." Her tone was confirming yet incredulous.

Maia shrugged, trying her best to look non-committal. "I met him at church," she stated nonchalantly. Anything to avoid talking about his affections.

"I know."

"He told you?" Maia asked, surprised.

"No, Derek is a very private person. Faith Life is a big church, but it's also a small church, if you get what I mean." Lian tucked her bone-straight black bob behind her ears, avoiding eye contact.

Maia could tell that there was much more Lian wasn't saying so she decided to push for more. Could it get any worse than the gossiping old ladies in the bathroom? "How bad is it, really?"

Though she had just met Lian, something about her eyes and demeanor told Maia she was trustworthy.

Lian caught her gaze and reached for her hand, covering it with hers. "People judge. It's second nature for most. It's easy to judge what you don't understand or come to a conclusion based only on appearances. Faith Life is an amazing church, but it's full of imperfect people, darling. Don't take the gossip of bored old women and misguided young ones to heart. I've been there, done that, and wrote a book about it. When James and I got together, they nearly tore us apart. He was a sexy, tattooed biker, and I was the deacon's daughter. It was scandalous."

Maia watched Lian's eyes glaze over as she spoke about her husband. The woman was head over heels for sure.

"But you know what that ordeal taught me? Opinions are just that. What matters most is what God thinks. Don't let people bully you with their opinions. I almost missed out on the love of my life because I cared too much about what others thought. Don't fall into that same trap," Lian finished, relinquishing Maia's hand and returning her attention to the game which had already resumed.

"Thank you," Maia replied. "I needed that."

Lian smiled warmly at her, nodded, and then promptly returned to viewing the game.

Maia tried to concentrate, but Lian's words reverberated in her mind for the rest of the second half. Before she knew it, the game was over and people trickled outside until the place was empty. As James locked up the gym, she accepted Derek's invitation to a light dinner with the other couple.

Chapter 12

Instead of traveling with Derek, Maia had opted to drive to the restaurant with Lian for "girl talk" as Lian put it. He trusted both James and Lian with his very life so he knew Maia was in safe company. That left Derek and James riding together for the short drive. It was not long before James broke the silence in the car.

"So…" he started.

"So, what?" Derek asked, already on the defensive. He sincerely hoped this would not turn into another lecture from someone he considered family.

"Touchy aren't we, mate? I was just going to say that Maia seems like a sweet girl."

"I'm sorry," Derek apologized quickly, "I've just had so many lectures from my parents already. I don't need another."

"Who am *I* to lecture *you*? Ex-cons who marry worship leaders don't get to judge," he said wryly. "I just want to make sure that you understand what you're getting yourself into. I know *you* don't care what people think, but the congregants probably won't give Maia an easy time of it."

"We're only just getting to know each other. It's a complicated situation Jay and I have no idea what I'm doing. I just know that I like Maia and I feel like God is in this. It doesn't make any sense, but when we're together, I feel a peace like I've never felt before."

They sat in silence for a few minutes before James spoke up.

"Well, mate, go for it...just protect her at all costs."

"I'll try even harder to do just that." Derek said determinedly.

Dinner was everything Maia needed to relax before the week ahead. The laughter and repartee made her feel like her old self again; young and carefree. They talked about everything under the sun and just like Derek, both Lian and James acknowledged her pregnancy, but did not seek to make her feel inferior because she was unmarried.

By the time Derek walked her to her apartment door, it was a little after eight and for the first time in many months, she was not tired. She unlocked her door and then turned to him, smiling.

"Thank you for a great evening, LeBron," Maia teased.

He laughed. "You got jokes, I see."

She chuckled.

"I really enjoy your company. I don't think I've ever had such easy-going conversations with a woman in my life."

Maia beamed, but refrained from relaying the same sentiments. "Thank you for getting me out of the apartment and thank you for the massage voucher. It was everything I needed."

"You're welcome."

"Have a wonderful night, Derek."

As she turned to go inside, she felt a soft touch on her arm.

"Maia, I'd like to see you again if that's okay with you. I'd like to cook lunch for you sometime."

She blushed. "I'd like that too."

"Okay," Derek nodded, beaming. "I'll message you when I get in and we can pick a day."

She nodded with a warm smile and finally bid him goodnight.

Before Maia knew it, almost a week had passed since her basketball date with Derek, yet still, she found it impossible to stop thinking about him. It was Friday and while she stood preparing dinner for herself and Destiny, her mind remained preoccupied. Every time she thought about his almost-perfect smile, her heart did small somersaults in her chest. He had taken to texting her throughout the day and they talked about everything under the sun. It was becoming increasingly difficult to avoid the conversation of her imminent transition to motherhood.

A few days before, Derek had inquired about what led her to Texas. After a long hesitation from her, he'd let her know that she could share when she felt ready, but he would need to know more about her before they could progress past friendship.

Logically, she had known this fork in the road was inevitable, but the idea of sharing that part of her life with Derek, scared her senseless. What if he decided she had too much baggage? The idea of losing him made her… She stopped the thought dead in its tracks. *Losing him?* How could she lose what she never had to begin with? That thought alone revealed the depth of her feelings. She had been telling herself that this was simply a friendship, but she knew her heart was already invested in Derek. It wouldn't be long before she would have to tell him everything, before her heart became even more entangled.

The fear that he wouldn't believe her or perhaps he would no longer want anything to do with her was the reason behind her hesitation. Regardless of the outcome, Maia knew he deserved the whole story before he committed to anything beyond friendship.

By the time the roasted potatoes and chicken she had in the oven was finished, Destiny was knocking on her door. Maia let her in, finally settling on opening up to Derek at their lunch date tomorrow. Destiny bustled through the door and made a beeline for the couch.

"Are you finally gonna tell me how your date went?" Maia called as she walked back to the kitchen.

"I don't want to talk about it," Destiny clipped.

"That bad, huh? I'm sorry lovey."

Destiny harrumphed and quickly changed the subject, inquiring about Lily.

"We are both fine. Come on, Des, give me something. What happened on the date?"

"I got stood up, okay?" she replied gruffly.

Maia winced. "I thought your friend said he was solid."

"Yeah, well maybe she doesn't know the guy as well as she thinks she does," Destiny snapped.

"I'm sorry, Des."

"For what? You weren't the one who stood me up. I just can't believe he wasted my time like that."

"I'm sure you'll find someone who won't waste your time," Maia reassured her.

"Yeah, maybe." Her words sounded anything but hopeful. "Enough about me, though. How are you and preacher boy?"

"We're good," Maia revealed, not wanting to add to her friend's load.

"Come on. Spill the beans. It's a welcomed distraction."

"Those *are* the beans."

Destiny rolled her eyes. "Chile, you think I don't know you by now?"

"Fine. We're having lunch tomorrow. I'm going to tell him what happened back in Jacksonville."

"You don't think it's too soon?"

"I don't think we can move forward unless we both open up about our pasts. He's been very transparent and he deserves the same, even if he chooses to walk away.

Her friend nodded and they settled into a pensive silence as Maia plated their food. Lily had been active all day and even now the movements were causing her slight discomfort. She began singing Lily's lullaby, hoping the melody would perform its usual magic.

"Have you signed up for the music ministry yet?" Des asked dubiously, fully aware that Maia had not.

"I'll do it after Lily is born."

Destiny had been encouraging her to audition for the music ministry from the very first moment she heard Maia sing.

"Will you be more forgiven after she's born?"

"No— but…I don't-I can't-I'm already on the radar for talking to Derek. I don't need any more judgment or scrutiny. Besides, I don't want anyone to think that I'm glorifying getting pregnant out of wedlock."

"Sounds like excuses to me, Maia."

She should be used to her friend's bluntness by now, but it still hit her as abrasively as it always had.

"Yes, very valid excuses," Maia stated, her tone conveying that the conversation would end there. She had been there and done that back in Jacksonville and she didn't think she would ever want to sing in church again anyway.

Just then, Destiny got up to help her bring the food to the table and they continued their girls' night with much lighter conversation.

Chapter 13

As Saturday dawned, Derek lay in his bed, talking to God. He'd finished his devotion time and now lay seeking the Lord for clarity on how he should proceed with Maia. The more he thought about his predicament, the less clear his path forward seemed to be.

He liked Maia, certainly, but the risk in committing to a relationship with her seemed so much greater than the potential reward. Anything could happen. Lily's father could come waltzing back into Maia's life at any moment for all he knew. What if she wasn't over him? Anxiety weighed like a brick on his heart. Derek took a deep breath and closed his eyes. He hadn't made any commitment yet, he reminded himself. There was no reason to feel this anxious.

Praying silently, he allowed God's peace to wash over him. Suddenly, he felt the presence of God strongly in his room and he immediately picked up the journal and pen he kept next to his bed. As was his custom in moments like this, he waited for the Lord to speak.

"I am giving you a family."

"Lord, I already have a family," he replied, his mind immediately flitting to his parents and plethora of extended relatives.

"Maia will be your wife and Lily, your daughter. I am giving you your own family."

Immediately, Derek dropped the pen like it was on fire and his heart began to race again. The Lord's voice was clear as day. Even as his heart continued its dance in his chest and he tried to wrap his mind around this revelation, Derek felt an immense relief from his earlier panic.

"Maia will be my wife," Derek said the words aloud. They sounded more unbelievable in the quiet of his room than they had in his head. Despite his shock, there was a deep *knowing* that these words were true and if he were honest with himself, from the very first moment he met Maia, he had known this truth. Even when his logical mind had fought the *knowing* tooth and nail, he had known.

Many "what-ifs" swirled in his mind, but even before he could express one of them, the Lord whispered to his heart again.

"You do not have to worry. I give good gifts. Trust Me to bring My word to pass. Trust that it will be good."

Derek immediately came to a resolve. "I will trust You, Lord," he whispered, meaning every word.

He lay a little while longer before he got up to begin preparations for lunch with his future wife. The thought alone ignited anticipation within him.

Later that afternoon, Maia and Derek sat comfortably at his dining table finishing the mac and cheese with fried chicken that he made. His massive rottweiler lay on his dog bed in the corner of the room, looking longingly at their plates ever so often. Maia wasn't an animal lover, but Zeke was docile enough. When she walked in, he sniffed her toes for a few seconds before deeming her wholly uninteresting. Besides the occasional yelp, you wouldn't even know he was there.

As she looked around Derek's dining room, she marveled at the beauty of the decor. The two-story country home had taken Maia aback. It was definitely too big for just one man. His brief tour revealed that there were at least five bedrooms. It was more beautiful than anything she had seen or experienced in Jacksonville, that's for sure.

"This is delicious, Derek. Your home is breathtaking as well," Maia commented, around her last mouthful of fried chicken.

"Thank you. My mama's recipe never fails. This meal is the best you're gonna get from me, though, I'm afraid. I'm a bit of a one trick pony in the kitchen," Derek chuckled.

"Regardless, thank you for your effort."

"You're welcome."

They engaged in their usual banter after the meal. Derek insisted on washing the dishes so she sat at the table while he completed the task. As they spoke across the granite island that separated them, she discovered that he invested in real estate which was the source of the majority of his income.

"I guess that would explain your choice of abode," she stated, laughing nervously.

Derek placed the last fork in the dish rack and turned to face her, leaning back against the counter while drying his hands with a nearby kitchen towel.

"I specifically purchased this home with the hope of having a family here," he responded, walking back over to the table where she was. "I'd like to be married one day and to be a father as well." He sat down.

"Oh." Maia wanted to say something else, *anything* else, but her mind was blank. She'd never met a man so sure of himself and what he wanted out of life. Sure, many talked the talk, but for him to purchase this home with his future in mind, it was admirable.

"Would you like to go out to the back porch? There's a beautiful view of The Peak from there."

"Sure." Maia had heard of the locally famed mountain, but had never seen it before.

Derek stood and held out his hand to her. Slipping her hand into his, Maia rose to her feet. She expected him to release her after she was standing, but his hand enveloped hers until they were seated on his wicker patio chair made for two. His wrap-around porch was beautifully decorated and added to the rustic feel of his home's exterior.

She could picture Saturday barbecues and kids running free in the large backyard. Her heart ached with desire for the picture to become a reality and the improbability of it made her want to cry. She turned her attention back to the man at her side and they sat quietly taking in the mountain view.

"I was thinking about—"

"Maia, there's something—"

They both spoke at the same time, then paused to laugh at the awkward moment.

"You go first," Derek said, still chuckling.

"I was thinking about what you said and I want to be open with you, I do. I just—I don't want to be hurt again. If you're not serious, please, I beg you, don't play with my heart."

She forced herself to meet his obsidian eyes. He needed to know that she was deeply serious.

"Oh Maia. I don't think I've been handling this well at all. I've been holding myself back because there's still so much that I don't know about you. If I'm being honest, those unknowns scare the heck out of me and that's partially because of my past and insecurities."

Derek took a deep breath and the story of him and Jessica poured from his lips. Maia sat quietly listening as he shared. As he finished speaking, his shoulders visibly relaxed.

"I've been holding back because this attraction between us seems so precarious at times, the future of it, I mean. When I was sixteen, the only future I could envision, was snatched away in an instant. I've healed and forgiven, but I don't think I could bear pain or loss like that again."

Maia's eyes widened at his confession. She understood his hesitancy and fear. They were not without reason. As she looked at him, she felt the walls around her heart crumbling without her permission. His vulnerability rested in the hunch of his shoulders and the many questions reflected in his eyes. Maia lifted her hand to cup his cheek, her thumb gently stroking his beard.

"I'm so sorry that happened to you, D. I can't even imagine what that must have been like. You deserve someone who will love you just as much as you love them. You deserve a love that stays."

She watched the play of emotions as they crossed his face. Surprise, admiration, and then a softness that she couldn't name. His Adam's apple worked furiously in his throat as he opened his mouth to speak and she realized he was holding back tears.

"Falling in love with you when I don't know if forever with you is even a possibility, seems foolish."

Maia's lips parted and the hand at his cheek slowly fell away as she thought about his words. She turned her gaze toward The Peak, wanting to look anywhere but in his eyes.

Suddenly, his finger was on her chin, turning her face toward his. His eyes captured hers with their intensity.

Maia's breath caught in her throat and she couldn't speak, even if she wanted to. The fire in his gaze silenced everything around them and for a moment, they were the only two people in the world. For a second she thought he might kiss her, but instead, he spoke the words that changed everything.

"And yet, here I am—falling anyway."

Maia's heart thumped in her chest and butterflies swirled in her stomach. Everything within her wanted to believe his words, but she had heard them before from lips that were as traitorous as the person attached to them. Immediately, she felt the conviction of the Holy Spirit. Derek was not Eli and he shouldn't have to pay for Eli's mistakes.

She closed her eyes and exhaled slowly. She too was falling in love, but before she could share her heart with Derek, she knew she had to be honest about her past.

"I've never told you why I moved to Texas, but I think it's time I share the full story…

Chapter 14

Jacksonville, Florida

Six months ago

"You can't be pregnant and if you are, it's not mine," Eli Carter said contemptuously. His eyes darted this way and that as they sat in his car at the park.

Maia's whole world stopped as the father of her child denied his responsibility.

"Eli, you know you were my first and I haven't been with anyone else," she replied, desperate for him to believe her.

"We used a condom."

"And condoms break… Eli, please. I'll do whatever you want. I'll take a DNA test, whatever you want. I promise you this baby is yours. We were going to get married any way, right? Let's just do it now."

"I was never going to marry *you*. You're not pastor's wife material. Never was, never will be. I don't know whose kid that is, but it ain't mine."

"Eli!" Maia cried in desperation, her eyes pleading with him to believe her. She searched his face for any semblance of the charming and flirtatious man who had romanced her for the past three months, but he was nowhere to be found. "Don't you care that I'm carrying your baby? What will you do when the baby comes out looking like you?" she asked, anger quickly overtaking her hysteria.

Eli faltered for a second and that second was all it took for Maia to see the truth written all over his face. He knew this baby was his, but wasn't going to admit it. The past three months flashed before her eyes. Without the idealistic tint of her rose-colored glasses, Eli's intentions became horribly apparent. She recalled his insistence upon "discretion". He'd convinced her it was to protect their relationship from church gossip, but she knew better now.

They'd texted for months and gone out a few times, but all those dates were on the outskirts of town where it was unlikely to run into anyone familiar. Her own naiveté made Maia want to slap herself. How could she have been so stupid?

"It's not mine and you'd be a fool to keep it." The hard planes of his face looked nothing like the Eli she thought she'd known. His callousness broke her heart and she saw her future play out before her, bleak and daunting.

"You're a coward. I promise you'll regret this one day," Maia spat. Slamming the car door, she ran to her truck, parked a few yards away from Eli's. She sat behind the wheel for another hour as sobs wracked her body.

The last three months played on loop in her brain. From the moment Eli had discreetly asked for her number after a young adult's ministry meeting, she should have known. In retrospect, all the signs of his true character were glaringly obvious. He had kept her a secret, not to avoid gossip, but because he never had any intention of marrying her to begin with.

Maia shuddered as she thought about the fact that she had given him her virginity in exchange for empty promises. She'd broken the promise she made to God at seventeen and had sex with a man who was not her husband. From the moment it had happened, Maia regretted it, and she refused to be alone with Eli again. But still, here she was, pregnant and alone. She had no plan and no idea what would happen next.

When her tears finally subsided, she started Ginger up and drove home. Dread filled her as she sat outside of her grandma's modest home. She'd lived here since she was six and it had always felt like a haven, but tonight, its fern green walls loomed like gallows before her.

"God, please help me," she whispered, even though He felt as far away as the sky at that moment.

There was no fanfare, no big sign in the sky to reassure her, but her anxiety eased and she felt like she could breathe. For the first time since she'd seen those two lines on that pregnancy test three days ago, she thought about the little life growing inside of her. Eli's words echoed in her ears, 'you'd be a fool to keep it'. Even as the thought crossed her mind, she knew instantly that she'd never be able to go through with a termination. That was not an option, no matter what Eli thought she should do. She rubbed her tummy softly, still finding it hard to believe there was a baby in there. In that moment, without a plan, without any idea how things would play out, she chose her baby. With that resolve, she locked up Ginger and prepared to face Mimi.

Nothing went according to plan. As she spoke, Mimi's plump face went from shock to disappointment and finally stopped at anger after she told her the baby was Eli's.

Mimi rose from the settee in the living room. "How dare you lie on the man of God!"

Maia's eyes flew up to her grandmother's in disbelief. She had seen Mimi in almost every state: happy, sad, tired, angry, and frustrated. However, the look of pure disgust in her eyes now, was something Maia had never experienced, something she surely never thought she'd be the recipient of. Mimi had shown Maia tough love all her life, but she'd never been cruel.

She tried in vain to convince Mimi of the truth, even pulling out her phone in an attempt to show her the text messages they'd shared, but Clarissa Miller refused to even look at them. After a few minutes of pleading through her tears, Maia resigned herself to her reality. There would be no getting through to Mimi tonight.

Maia lived the next week on autopilot. She trudged to work each day in a daze of depression, only to come home to tense and awkward silence from Mimi. Every time Maia passed by her grandmother in the house, she could not help but notice the looks of judgment.

By the time Sunday rolled around, desperation prompted Maia to seek out Pastor Carter after church. She waited around until there were only a handful of people left in the sanctuary and then approached the pastor. Wasting no time beating around the bush, her confession quickly turned into a meeting in his office. He called both Eli and Clarissa into the office after everyone else had gone home.

As things unfolded, Maia couldn't help but feel like she was living in a nightmare. It felt like the people who stood before her, who had known her almost her whole life, had suddenly become strangers. Eli denied ever even dating her, Mimi apologized profusely for raising "a liar and a heathen", and Pastor Carter sided with his son. Maia felt like her entire world was collapsing and she could do nothing to stop it.

Everything that happened after that seemed like a blur. As they walked out of the meeting, Mimi turned an icy glare upon her.

"I want you out of my house by tomorrow. I didn't raise you to be a liar, but clearly, you're your mother's child." Those were the last words Mimi said to her.

Maia wasted no time in packing her meager belongings into her truck that day. It took all of an hour. She drafted her resignation from the tech company where she worked and began a journey as far as Ginger would take her.

Chapter 15

A touch on her cheek brought Maia back to the present. She'd gotten so lost in her story and didn't realize tears were streaming down her face. Derek's thumb gently rubbed her other cheek as he wiped the tears away.

"I'm sorry. I don't know why I'm still crying all this time later."

"You never have to apologize for feeling, Maia. You're allowed to feel."

"I thought I was in love, but that was just infatuation. I'm moving forward, Derek. There's no need for you to worry. Even if by some miracle he decides to take responsibility, I have no desire to rekindle a relationship with him. I did not take my repentance lightly and I don't intend on making the same mistakes again."

"I'm sorry, Maia. Neither Lily nor you deserve that kind of cowardice."

"I've forgiven him and I understand that he's just not mature enough to take responsibility. God has given me immeasurable grace to handle it all. Lily will have everything that she needs. I believe that with all of my being. The part that still hurts so much is how things ended with my Mimi. That's been the most difficult part. I thought she knew me. It hurt so much when she believed Eli over me. It *still* hurts."

"I can't even imagine how difficult that was for you."

"My mom and I lived with Mimi until I was six. That's when mom left. She had me so young and my father was never around. I don't think she was prepared for all the responsibility. She'd pop in on my birthday each year, but even *that* stopped when I was sixteen. The point is, Mimi has been the only mother I've known for most of my life. Sometimes I still can't believe she trusted Eli more than she did me."

Derek reached over and placed his hand on Maia's. "That would devastate anyone, Maia, and you didn't deserve the kind of pain that you endured. To not be believed by the person who raised you *is* a hurtful thing. I want you to know that I'm here for you. Anytime you need to talk, I'm here."

"It's just nice to have someone to share the load with. That's more than enough."

Derek nodded and they both allowed their burdens to hang in the silence and it dawned on Maia, that with Derek, she didn't need all the answers. It was enough just to sit in the comfort of his presence while things were still falling into place.

In a moment of sheer bravado, she reached across, intending on placing her lips to his cheek. At the very moment she leaned in, Derek turned his head and their lips collided.

Maia pulled away like his lips were a hot iron. They looked at each other in shock for a few seconds before they busted out in laughter at the sheer awkwardness of the moment. It was the type of laughter that caused stitches.

"At least buy me dinner first," Derek teased, barely getting the words out.

She smacked him playfully on his arm, pretending to pout.

"That's one heck of a first kiss, Ms. Miller," he quipped.

"It was less of a kiss and more of a…lip smash," Maia giggled.

"Do I get a do-over?" he asked, entwining his hand with hers.

"Yeah, yeah you do."

"I'll make sure to choose the right time. After all, we only get one first kiss." Derek lifted their joined hands and pressed his lips to her smooth, caramel skin there.

She smiled as she looked up at him, hopeful for the future, yet tentative with her joy. He released her hand and sighed heavily before he spoke.

"Come on. Let's get you home before it gets too late."

Maia hated that Des' romantic life seemed to be sinking even deeper in the trenches while she was experiencing the exact opposite. If it were possible to build a man for her friend, she would. Nevertheless, she offered the next best thing, a listening ear to Des' dating escapades.

Her latest attempts at dating had led her to a popular Christian dating app and she now sat recapping a disastrous date that included hibachi, a fire extinguisher, and a suggestive invite back to his apartment. Though unfortunate, Destiny's retelling of events was hilarious and Maia tried unsuccessfully to hide her bemusement.

"So, you're covered in ammonium phosphate and he's still propositioning you? Where do you find these men, Des?"

"The dating streets may as well be the streets of hell, girl. It's depressing."

"What about the blind date guy that stood you up? Did he at least apologize?" Maia asked.

Destiny looked at her curiously. "He did, actually. Reagan gave him my number, without my permission, might I add. As far as I'm concerned, 'cold feet' is not a reason to stand someone up, so I shot him down for date number two. Besides, Reagan showed me a picture of him after I told her and he's white with salt and pepper hair." Destiny gave her a dubious stare. "Now you *know* I'm all for interracial romance, but I myself prefer my coffee black, thank you very much."

"Don't block your blessings, now. That's all I'm saying."

"He's old!" Destiny shrieked.

Maia cackled.

"He's like forty! I'm not even joking."

"Forty is *not* old, Destiny René," Maia chided.

"Either way, I shot him down. And I've moved on."

"Okay, okay," Maia acquiesced. "I wish I could make a man for you. I would if I could," she added seriously.

"If only it worked like that! Don't worry about me, Maia. I'm honestly so happy that you are happy. I can't think of anyone who deserves it more. That being said, are you prepared to 'hashtag meet the parents' this weekend?"

"Uggh, no I'm not. We've been living in our own little bubble for the past couple of weeks and it has been surreal. I don't want to ruin it with reality. They're *his* parents, after all. I'm just the knocked-up girl who's dating their son. They're probably going to chase me as far away from Texas as they can."

"Derek's an adult. He can make his own choices. They may not approve, but they're not the ones in the relationship," Destiny responded, while shrugging nonchalantly.

She made it sound so easy, Maia thought. When Derek had invited her to lunch at his parents this weekend, her decline had been instant. It had taken three days for her to finally come around and she had only done so because it was important to Derek that they have his parents' blessing.

Maia spent the next few days dreading the interaction. She reminded herself again that Derek was worth the effort. He kept surprising her with his patience and understanding, so lunch with his parents was the least she could do.

Chapter 16

Derek wiped his forehead for the tenth time in as many minutes. His parents had been firing questions at Maia since the moment they ended grace, fifteen minutes ago. He could tell Maia was uncomfortable so he cleared his throat.

"Mom, dad, please. Let Maia breathe, will you? This isn't the rapid-fire segment of a game show."

"We're just trying to get to know her," his mother replied pointedly.

"Yeah, well, not by interrogating her like she committed a crime—"

"I am happy to tell you more about myself," Maia interrupted.

Derek and his mother fell silent before Maia continued speaking. She told them just enough about her upbringing without going into too much detail. It was obvious to Derek that she was intentionally attempting to charm the socks off of his parents and by the time she finished speaking, southern propriety would not allow Carl and Coretta Hunter to ask any further questions throughout their meal.

By the time the evening was over, his parents had completely warmed to Maia; though he knew nothing but time, would completely allay their fears. His mother had taken a few moments alone with her for "girl talk" as she put it. Derek stood in the living area only half-listening to his father talk about a basketball game. His eyes kept darting across the room to where his mother and Maia sat. None of their words reached his ears, but the intensity in their eyes set off alarm bells in his head. Just when he was about to excuse himself and break up their conversation, his mother's shoulders relaxed and she smiled warmly, embracing Maia in a hug. He could not even pretend to be paying attention to his father anymore.

"I've never seen you like this with anyone, son," Carl's voice pierced the fog of his distraction and his eyes found his father's.

"What do you mean?"

"It's like you two are connected by some invisible string. You sense her without seeing her. I've observed you all evening and it's like you're communicating without words. She moves, you move. She gets nervous, you perk up."

Derek simply looked at his father, waiting for an explanation of the worry that laced Carl's voice.

"It's been such a short time. How can you be so sure about this?"

"I wish I had a good enough answer for you, dad. I had my reservations too, but God has been so present throughout this entire thing. I have no doubt that this is the Lord's doing and I know I have His approval. She's the one."

Carl's eyes widened and just then his mother's voice interrupted the conversation.

"What are you two going on about over there? You look like you're deciding the fate of all mankind." She walked over to Carl as she spoke and smoothed his furrowed brow with her thumb and index finger. "Relax your face, dear. What have I told you about frowning so much?"

Carl looked put out by her interruption, but he simply nodded.

Derek knew that the conversation was just tabled until a more opportune time, but he breathed a sigh of relief anyway. His eyes drifted to Maia and though she was smiling, her eyes spoke of tiredness.

"Are you ready to skedaddle?" he asked softly.

She nodded discreetly as his parents moved toward the couch.

Derek quickly made excuses and they said their 'goodbyes'. When they reached the car, he patted his pockets trying to locate his keys only to find that they were empty. He dashed inside to retrieve them from their usual resting spot on his parent's coffee table, but not before Carl cornered him in the hallway. While his dad did not pretend to understand Derek's certainty about the relationship, he reassured his son that he trusted his judgment. His dad's assurance meant the world to him and in an uncharacteristic show of affection, he hugged the old man.

His father's eyes widened as Derek released him and Carl cleared his throat uncomfortably. "This girl *must* be special for my son to be giving out hugs."

Derek rolled his eyes, but still smiled with sheepish chagrin. He said goodbye again and drove Maia to her apartment, walking her to her door as he always did.

"Would you like to come in?" Maia asked, turning the key to unlock her apartment door.

"No thanks, it's pretty late."

She nodded, understanding all of his unspoken reasons. Propriety and conviction would not allow him to stay.

"Well, thank you for standing up for me tonight. You look out for me in a way I've never known. I appreciate it, D…more than you know.

"It's nothing, Sunshine."

He'd given her the nickname a couple of weeks ago and without fail, it made her heart skip a beat each time he used it.

"There *is* one thing I've been wanting to ask you for a few days." He lounged languidly in her doorway, bracing his muscled arm on the door frame for support. Despite his attempt at nonchalance, his eyes told the truth of his nervousness. They shifted fervently from hers to the floor as she waited for him to continue. "I wanted to ask—that is—I wanted to know if you would—if we could—" Derek stammered.

Maia chuckled nervously. "Are you okay?"

He nodded, but still continued to stutter helplessly until he finally blurted out the only coherent thing he'd said in the past five minutes. "Will you be my girlfriend?"

Maia stood with her lips agape. **Surprised** was an understatement of how she was feeling. His question set her skin ablaze with an unfamiliar heat and her heart thumped violently in her chest. Yet, she knew her answer would be yes, undoubtedly and unequivocally yes.

Despite her resolution, she could not help but make him sweat a little. She stood stoic, her expression betraying none of her feelings. "Why do you want me to be your girlfriend?" Her eyes met his.

He hesitated only a moment before answering. "Because I see a real future with you. I didn't realize how guarded and lonely I was until you came along, Mai. You add laughter and softness to my life, things I didn't know I needed. It's the little things that draw me to you. The other day when I picked you up from work, I saw you run to the alley outside the cafe to give food and money to a homeless woman. What struck me is that you didn't do it to be seen. You had no idea I was watching. Your kindness is just one of the many reasons why I'd like you to be mine. I want to add to your life, to take care of you in every way that matters. So, if you would have me, I'd love to be yours."

Maia knew in that moment, as surely as she knew the sky was blue, that she was falling in love with this man. Fast and hard, the kind of fall that would be almost impossible to recover from. It scared her, but it also made her feel exhilaratingly free. She wanted to fling her arms around him and scream her "yes" from the rooftops, but she refrained.

She simply nodded and smiled at him cheesily. "Okay. I'll think about it and let you know soon."

Derek nodded slowly, his hand moving from the door frame to the pocket of his jeans. Rocking back on his heel, he exhaled and then spoke. "Well, I know you're probably tired so I should get going. Thank you for agreeing to meet my parents. It meant a lot to me." He smiled and gave her one final nod before turning to leave.

Before she could quell the impulse, her hand reached out to him, resting gently on his forearm to stop him from leaving. There was no logical explanation for why that small touch felt so different from all the others that had gone before, but as he turned again toward her, the air between them felt charged. And before cowardice could claim her, the truth spewed from her lips. "I've had time to think and…" Her eyes met his intently.

Curiosity and fear played on his face until curiosity finally won out.

Taking a deep breath, she offered her answer. "I'd be honored to be your girlfriend," Maia finished soberly.

Derek's eyes widened in surprise before his shoulders slumped in relief. "Are you sure?" His eyes searched hers for any doubt.

"As sure as I'll ever be."

His eyes captured hers and they stood for what felt like hours before he took a small step toward her, bringing himself closer. Maia's breath quickened and she knew instinctively that he was going to kiss her. That thought alone made breathing impossible. Derek lifted his hands to softly frame her face before leaning in to press his lips to hers.

Though Maia had wondered what his kisses would feel like, nothing prepared her for the softness of his lips nor the liquid fire that burned hot in her blood as his lips explored hers. Before she knew it, her arms were linked around his neck and her lips parted to allow his thorough exploration. Without her permission, a soft whimper formed in her throat and all too soon, Derek dragged his lips away from hers and took an exaggerated step backward. His eyes were ablaze with some unnamed emotion, but he flashed her a wide smile and the fire disappeared just as quickly. Suddenly, she felt incredibly shy in his presence and wished she could somehow hide from her handsome mountain of a man. Just then, his voice interrupted her thoughts.

"How was that for a first kiss?" he asked, searching her eyes for the answer.

"Five stars on Kiss Advisor."

He laughed loudly and in an exaggerated motion, he tipped an imaginary hat and gave a bow. They both chuckled and then Derek spoke again. "So, you've met the parents."

"Yes, I have, and it wasn't as bad as I thought it would be."

"My parents love you, even if they *are* still apprehensive about us," he reassured her.

"So, what's next, D?"

His face immediately became serious and the intensity she saw in his eyes drew her in. "I'm in this, Maia. We can take things at whatever pace you're comfortable with, but I'm serious about you. And forever is what I have in mind."

Maia's heart melted. Her experience with Derek was so different from her encounters with Eli. This man was not trying to hide her nor was he using ambiguous language. She never had to wonder where she stood with him because he was so open with her. Before she could talk herself out of it, she reached up and flung her arms around him, planting her face in his chest to hide the tears that were threatening.

"Thank you," she cried, her voice muffled in his t-shirt.

"What's this for?" There was a measure of softness in his voice that she had never heard from him before this moment. He rubbed her back softly, waiting for her answer.

"You've given me something I forced myself to stop dreaming of. When I moved here, I had no idea what God had in store for me, but I'm so glad it was you. I couldn't ask for anything more."

Derek clasped her even more tightly and they stayed that way for a few minutes before they finally said their goodbyes and he left.

Chapter 17

<hr>

Maia spent most of that night smiling dreamily on her bed. Though the dinner had started awkwardly, her chat with Coretta really put her at ease. After explaining that she didn't want to see her son get hurt, she asked Maia why she was even dating, given her being almost eight months pregnant and all. Maia had given the question some thought before responding as honestly as she could.

Ultimately, when she moved to Texas, the last thing on her mind was dating. Derek Hunter had been a beautiful and frightening surprise. If it weren't for Destiny's continual nudges of encouragement and God's reminders that her past, no matter how evident, should not disqualify her from happiness, she wouldn't have given him the time of day. In their nightly chats since having lunch at his place, he always included Lily when he talked of the future and Maia could tell that her daughter would not be a concession for him, but a welcomed addition to his life.

All she could do was vehemently assure Coretta that she would treat Derek with the same respect and care that he gave to her. The truth was that he seemed an anomaly in a world full of Elis and it was easy for her to tell Coretta why she liked him. After her long-winded gushing, the plump older woman had embraced and reassured her that she would support them because she trusted her son to make wise decisions. That was all Maia could ask for until his parents got to know her better.

She tried to quiet her many thoughts so she could get some sleep, to no avail. Instead, she picked up her guitar and began to write a love song. For the first time in a long time, she felt inspired and she went with the flow of her creativity. It reminded her of a part of her life she had shared only with Destiny. Being a worship leader had been such a big part of her life in Jacksonville. Worship team rehearsals on Tuesdays and Thursdays, and choir rehearsals on Fridays. She loved singing, but it had been more of a burden than a calling before she moved. Returning to it felt daunting. She liked that here, in Texas, she was just Maia. In the months since she arrived, she'd rediscovered her passion for writing and singing. It felt like something she needed to fiercely protect.

Maia hadn't even told Derek about her love for music. Perhaps it felt too personal. She'd open up to him eventually, she promised herself. Until then, Lily would be her only audience. She wrote a light, fun verse and a catchy hook before sleep beckoned. Pushing her guitar and notebook to one side of the bed, she turned her bedside lamp off and quickly slipped into a peaceful slumber.

The next three weeks passed by in a blissful blur. Derek insisted on taking her to and from work each day since Ginger had taken to sputtering for a minimum of five minutes before her engine would come to life begrudgingly. They fell into a comfortable routine that felt anything *but* routine. Maia cooked and packed lunch for him each day of the week and she reveled in the compliments he gave after tasting each meal. Some of their evenings were spent praying together via video calls or having ridiculously hilarious conversations about everything and nothing.

In a show of defiance, she insisted on driving Ginger to church each Sunday in an attempt to retain some measure of independence. Despite Derek's invitation to accompany him, she usually sat with Destiny on Sundays to protect him from slander and she had a sneaky suspicion he did not protest because he was protecting *her*. She was sure rumors were still swirling, but no one dared approach her. Derek had spoken to the elders at their last meeting, assuring them of his moral standing. Though their courtship was unorthodox, as far as they were concerned, they owed explanations to no one else.

Every day, she thanked God for him. Things were moving so fast; her head was spinning. She could never have imagined that she would be in a relationship with a man of God who was proud to have her and who wanted to marry her. They'd grown so much closer over the past month. She knew when he was stressed by the way he held his shoulders and he could easily detect what she was feeling, simply by the cadence of her voice. It was all Maia hoped for in a man and everything about their relationship felt right.

Today, they sat, enjoying a picnic in the park. Though the weather was unpredictable at this time of the year and the city stood on the precipice of fall, warm days like today were still the norm. Maia had come today, prepared to share more of herself with Derek and that she *did*. She serenaded Derek with a familiar song about smiling through the tough times. After she was finished, he sat shell-shocked on the blanket they laid on.

"You've been holding back on me, Sunshine. All this time you've been hiding Christina Aguilera in your throat?"

She smiled shyly. "Well, I've been waiting for the right time. Today felt like the right time."

"Do you want to sing professionally?"

"I've never thought about it, really. I only ever sang in church. Maybe one day I'll pursue it, but I'm not ready."

"Your voice is beautiful regardless. That kind of beauty shouldn't be hoarded. It's meant to be shared; I think. But...all things in time."

She'd never thought about it that way, but his perspective was still not sufficient to coax her out of her shell so she just smiled and nodded.

"Since we're sharing, there's something I've been meaning to tell you." His body tensed, causing Maia to perk up.

"What is it?" she inquired.

"Uhh…a few months ago, my dad asked me to take over as lead pastor after he retires at the end of the year."

Maia tried to mask her many feelings about his confession in favor of gaining clarity. "Are you considering it?"

"More like wrestling with it. I don't want to disappoint my dad, but pastoring is not something I ever wanted to do. I want to help men. That's what I'm passionate about."

"Have you prayed about it?"

"More than I've prayed about anything in my life. This is the first time I feel like God hasn't given me an answer. I don't know what to do."

"Well let's pray about it together," Maia replied, taking his hand in hers.

They held hands and prayed for guidance, right there in the park. Afterward, Maia assured him that she would support him in whatever decision he would eventually make. He embraced her tightly and started to speak.

"I love—"

Maia's eyes shot up and she felt Derek's entire body tense before he continued.

"I love that I can depend on you to support me. It means so much to me."

"That's what we do for each other."

"How would *you* feel about me pastoring?"

Maia paused for a long time, thinking through her response before speaking.

"I think it's a huge responsibility and you'd eventually have to choose between having a hands-on role at Pidyon and being senior pastor at Faith Life. I think trying to do both would run you ragged. Ultimately, I want you to obey God. I'll support whatever decision you make and we'll navigate either path together."

Derek leaned in and pressed his lips to her forehead. "Thank you, sweetheart, but how do *you feel?*"

Maia sighed. The absolute last thing she wanted was to be a pastor's wife, least of all a 'pregnant-out-of-wedlock-for-someone-other-than-the-pastor' pastor's wife. At the same time, she knew that if Derek chose to take that path, she would adjust. He was the man of her dreams, the man she was sure God wanted her to be with. If the Lord led him into ministry, then He would grace her to handle the responsibility and scrutiny. Despite her faith, she still dreaded what she knew would be a gargantuan duty.

"I can't lie to you, D. Being a pastor's wife would not be my ideal future. I've been in church for many years and I've seen how harshly pastors and their families are judged and how overworked they often are. That's not a life I imagined for myself or my family. That being said, if God leads us to it, I know He'll give us the grace to handle everything that comes our way."

"Thank you for being honest. I plan to share the rest of my life with you, Mai, and your opinion matters to me. I'll continue to pray about it. I promise I'll let you know the moment I know what my decision will be."

She nodded and the two spent the rest of the evening talking about lighter and happier things, like how Lily had finally turned, allaying their fears of her having a C-section. With just a few weeks to go before her due date, Maia was brimming with excitement to meet her little girl and surprisingly, so was Derek. He seemed eager to welcome her into the world and from their lengthy conversations each night, she knew he was more than willing to be a father to Lily. Every night she went to sleep and every morning as she awoke, gratitude filled her heart. Somehow, God had taken the million broken pieces of her life and made something beautiful out of it.

Chapter 18

⬦

Just one week later, Maia stood in a baby store at the mall with Destiny. They'd popped into the store to grab a few last-minute things for Lily's arrival. Over the past few months, she'd been able to acquire almost everything she needed. Derek had gifted her the most beautiful crib and Des bought enough clothes to outfit her daughter for at least a year.

"My goddaughter deserves the best," she declared as she lugged eight bags filled to the brim into Maia's apartment. Onesies, booties, bibs, blankets, and cute outfits that had probably cost her friend a fortune had been included.

Maia purchased almost everything else she would need with the exception of breast pumps which brought her and Des to the busy mall this Saturday afternoon. It had not been long before Maia noticed that her bestie was not her usual talkative self. After paying for the pumps, they walked leisurely through the mall, chatting as they went.

"What's going on, girl? You're awfully quiet today," Maia noted.

Des released a heavy sigh. "I went on a date with Luke last week and things got a bit…heated."

Maia came to a dead stop, eyebrows raised in disbelief. "Whoa, whoa, whoa! Who the heck is Luke? I'm gonna need you to start from the beginning!" Maia squealed, pulling her friend toward the nearby fountain in the center of the mall. They sat on a bench in front of the fountain and Des started to explain.

"Luke is *salt and pepper guy*."

"I thought you were done with him after your botched blind date?"

"We started texting after his apology. He's sweet…and sexy in an unassuming kinda way," Destiny confessed, rolling her eyes at how corny she sounded. "He asked me out again and I said 'yes'. We had such a great time, Maia. I got a flat tire on my way out of the restaurant parking lot and he changed it, right there in his suit and followed me home to make sure I got there safely." Des relayed the story, interjecting an old-fashioned swoon with every point.

"This man must have an unrivaled gift of gab. I didn't think you were capable of swooning," Maia retorted sardonically.

"He's not a pushover. You know I give lip but he stands up to me and I don't know…I kinda like that."

"So, when you said 'things got heated', you meant that you had an argument?"

Destiny shook her head and Maia waited for her to continue. After it was clear that her friend had no plans on filling in the blanks, Maia held up her hands in surrender.

"Okay, where is my friend and what have you done with her? Usually, I can't get you to shut up, but getting this story out of you is like pulling teeth!"

Destiny rolled her eyes.

"I invited him in after he saw me home, okay? One minute we were arguing about how contentious I am and the next, well, we were kissing and hands were places they shouldn't be."

"Destiny René! Why am I only now hearing about this?" Maia shrieked.

"I wanted to tell you but you were having Braxton Hicks last week and I didn't want to add to your plate."

"You're not a burden, Des. There's always room on my plate for you," she giggled.

"Thank you," Des smiled. "I've been in a tizzy! That night, he stopped things, apologized, and I haven't heard from him since. No text, call, nor smoke signal. Heck! At this point, I'd settle for carrier pigeons. I texted him but…crickets."

Maia frowned. "I don't know about this guy, Des. From what you've told me, he seems kind of flaky. This is the second time he's gone ghost and you don't deserve that."

Destiny's face fell. "Logically, I know that, but there's something about him, Maia. I feel like I'm missing an integral piece of the puzzle here. If he would just open up…"

"Oh Des…you can't force him to do something he's not ready to do. Maybe he needs time. You've been abstinent for three years, girl. Don't compromise that for anyone. I'm a walking lesson of how *that* could go. I'm not saying he's wrong for you, but just proceed with caution. You deserve to be treated like a queen and I won't let you settle for anything less. He's got one more strike before I take my earrings out and fight him."

Des cackled, casting an incredulous look at Maia's rounded belly. "I don't think you'll be fighting anyone for a while, ma'am, but I know you want what's best for me and you're right. I'll give Luke his space and I'll stay away from him because chile, I lose my head when he's around," Des sighed, fanning herself.

Laughing, Maia gave her friend a side hug before they made their way to Des' car.

Later that evening, after Destiny had gone home, Maia sat on her couch nursing a cup of hot chocolate while watching a game show, when a knock at the door startled her. She watched the mug slip from her hands as if in slow motion. Yet, she was unable to stop the disaster that followed. The dark beverage hit her stomach and then fell to her lap, soaking through the floral maxi dress she was wearing. Immediately, the semi-hot liquid scorched her skin and she stood as quickly as she could manage, holding the wet dress away from her skin. She waddled awkwardly to the door while still holding the dress askew. She wasn't expecting Derek for a couple of hours, but she was always happy to see him.

"Well, somebody's earl—" she started, pulling the door open. Her words trailed off into nothingness and her jaw dropped. A million emotions swirled in her chest as she stood face to face with a familiar face. "Eli! What are you doing here?"

Derek pulled up to Maia's apartment and managed to cop the last parallel parking spot. He was early, but he had found himself sitting at home missing Maia, and had finally decided to surprise her with a treat from her favorite bakery. Cannoli in tow, he made his way to her apartment and knocked lightly on the door.

When the door opened, Derek stood face to face with a man he had never seen before. Though he was shorter than Derek, he was stalky in body with austere features. His naturally downturned lips set his face in a permanent scowl.

"Hello," Derek ventured tentatively.

Seconds ticked on and the man showed no signs of speaking. He raised an eyebrow, seemingly waiting for Derek to continue.

"Is Maia at home?" Derek asked, peering his head beyond the man's shoulder.

"Who's asking?" The stranger adjusted his body, blocking the inside of the apartment.

Immediately, Derek straightened his back, unfurling from his slumped posture so he stood at his full height. He leveled his eyes on the man whom he'd already decided he didn't like. "I'm Derek. Who are you?" he returned coolly.

Before the insolent stranger could retort, Maia's voice called out loudly from somewhere in the apartment. "I'll be right out, Eli! Changing clothes is complicated when you're pregnant."

The words struck Derek like bullets to the chest. His head swirled with all of the distressing possibilities of his discovery and he could hear his heart beating furiously in his ears. The entire ordeal felt like a nightmare. Every fear he had relegated to the far recesses of his mind, rushed to the fore. Like a hammer, they collided with his heart and instantly, he was sixteen again, hearing the worst news of his life.

Eli's lips curled in a sardonic grin and Derek wanted to punch the look of smugness from his face. He clenched his fist, ready to do just that, when Eli spoke again.

"As you can tell, we're a bit busy." The suggestiveness was not lost on Derek. He wanted to tackle the bastard until the anger and hurt he felt were nothing but a distant memory, but before he could act, Eli shut the door in his face.

Derek bit his fist, fury spreading heat over the length of his body. It was all he could do to stop himself from tearing the door off its hinges and beating Eli to a pulp. Before he did something he might regret, Derek turned on his heel and charged to his car. Speeding off in a plume of dust, he berated himself for his own naiveté. After reaching his driveway, Derek had no recollection of the journey that led him there. All he could think about was how stupid he had been all these months and how his heart was breaking into a million pieces.

Chapter 19

Maia emerged from her bedroom clad in the only maternity jeans she owned and an oversized T-shirt. The hot chocolate had given her a small, splotchy burn at the top of her tummy. It still seared, but barely so. Her eyes landed upon Eli.

"I could have sworn I heard you talking to someone," she muttered as she rounded the sofa and took a seat.

"Some guy named Derek. From the looks of his jealousy, I can see that it didn't take you very long to move on," Eli offered, his voice laced with accusation.

Maia released a shaky breath. God knows what Derek must have thought, finding Eli there. Why did Eli have to show up today of all days? She ignored his provocation and asked the question that had been on her mind from the moment she saw him at her door. "How did you find me?"

"I'd been scouring the internet for weeks, looking for any trace of you when I finally remembered that you were still sharing your phone's location with me."

Maia nodded. "Why are you here, Eli? You made it very clear you want nothing to do with me or your child."

"Don't act like you don't know why," he snapped, not even bothering to deny that Lily was his anymore. "Having this *child* is stupid." His mouth moved around the word contemptuously.

"You are a brute of a man. How could you be so heartless? Did you just come here to insult me and disown our child all over again?" Maia inwardly chided herself for ever believing any of the falsehoods that fell from his lips.

Eli sighed loudly and moved across the room to sit on the sofa as well. He took a deep, labored breath and spoke again. "Emotions are high, but I don't want there to be any bad blood between us, Maia. Let's start over. I came here to *help* you."

She acknowledged his words with a nod, waiting for him to explain himself.

Pulling a stuffed envelope out of his back pocket, he palmed it gingerly. "Are you planning on settling in Texas?" he inquired, his eyes never moving from the envelope.

"Why are you asking?" Maia asked warily.

"I just wanted to know. I—uh, I've taken over as youth pastor at the church and I wanted to help you get settled out here." He held out the envelope to her as he said the words, his eyes never quite meeting hers.

Maia's heart broke again, not because she had any shred of feeling within her for the man, but she wished she had given her daughter a more honorable father. She cast a glance at the envelope, but made no move to take it. "I don't want your *hush money*, Eli. You don't have to worry; I have no intention of moving back to Jacksonville and I certainly have no desire to tell anyone back in Florida that I was ever impregnated by the likes of *you*." Contempt laced each of her words as she ground them out.

Eli stood again. "I should have known better than to try and reason with an insipid little girl like you. You recruited that old biddy you call a grandmother to threaten me and now you want to pretend that you don't want my money?"

Her breath caught in her throat and confusion marred her face as she tried to make sense of his words. "Mimi threatened you?"

"Like you didn't put her up to it! She demanded I take care of my responsibilities or she would tell everyone that I have an illegitimate child."

"Mimi threatened you?" she repeated weakly.

Understanding dawned in Eli's eyes. "You didn't know?" His words were more statement than question.

"I-I…" Maia wanted to say something–anything, but her tongue clung to the roof of her mouth. What could she say? Somewhere along the line, Mimi had a change of heart. A dam inside her broke and tears rushed to her eyes. Maia let her eyelids flutter close, not wanting Eli to see any sign of weakness in her.

The vindication she felt as she thought of Mimi coming to her defense, felt so incredibly freeing. She immediately sat up straight and with a bravado she didn't have before, her eyes met Eli's. "I do not want your money, Eli. It's clear that you only care about yourself and protecting your reputation. I only hope you see the error of your ways before it's too late." Rubbing her stomach, she continued, "I allowed you to treat me like a dirty little secret you could sweep under the rug, but I'll be damned if I let you do it to my daughter. She'll know that she's wanted and celebrated and I will give her all the love she deserves." The tears she had been successfully holding back finally spilled onto her cheeks and she wiped them away furiously.

Eli's face fell for just a split second and she saw a cloak of shame shadow his features. However, it left just as quickly as it arrived. In its place was an unwavering determination. "Listen Maia, take the money and I'll be out of your hair. Clearly you need it if you're living in this hellhole." With one hand, he held out the envelope again and with the other, he waved in a vague motion referencing her apartment.

"I don't want your money, Eli. I have no desire to ruin you so you can go in peace. I forgive you and I want nothing from you." Reaching a place of resignation, Maia got up to escort him out of her life for good. He hesitated for a second more before he followed her. As she shut the door on her past with finality, she acknowledged that Eli was a hardened soul and nothing she said would change that. She found herself being grateful for his rejection eight months ago. Next to Lily, that was the greatest gift Eli had given her.

Maia stood in the silence of her apartment and all she could think about was Derek. God knows what Eli had said to him or what was going through his mind right now. Dialing his cell, she let the phone ring until the voicemail took over. She hung up without leaving a message. Trying his landline twice more with no success, she finally made up her mind to give him the space he needed to think.

Instead of worrying about something she could do nothing about at the moment, she picked up the phone again. This time, she dialed Mimi's number and waited with bated breath as it rang. However, when she heard her grandmother's voice, all of her bravery faded. After an awkwardly long silence, she said hello.

"Oh baby! I'm so glad to hear your voice."

"You are?" Maia asked, surprised.

"I've wanted to call you for weeks but I-I didn't know how I could ever face you after what I did. I'll never forgive myself for not believing you. I put you out *knowing* you had nowhere else to go. I was so cruel—" Clarissa's voice broke as she tried to get the words out.

Mimi's words broke her like nothing else could and tears rushed freely from Maia's eyes. "I forgive you, Mimi. I'm sorry for disappointing you. I only ever wanted to make you proud."

All of the hurt she felt poured from her eyes and her lips simultaneously as she poured out her heart.

They talked for over an hour, exchanging apologies and all that had transpired in the months since Maia left Florida. By the time she hung up, her heart was full. She looked forward to a promised visit from Mimi after Lily was born and judging by the frequency of the Braxton Hicks she was having, that would be any day now. Her heart filled with gratitude as she thought about the Lord's faithfulness. She could not have anticipated this chapter of her life. She'd been a hopeless wreck when she moved to Texas, but in God's sovereignty and mercy, He had worked it all for her good.

As she prepared for bed, prayers lifted from her lips to God's ears. She prayed for everyone in her life and in a moment of vulnerability she prayed that she would not lose the first and only man she ever wanted to love. He would undoubtedly be at church tomorrow and so, she texted Destiny to arrange transportation and then tried to get some sleep. As she drifted off, Maia was certain that everything would work out the way it should.

Chapter 20

As the sun eased its way above the horizon and light peeked through the windows in his room, Derek checked the time on his phone and turned off the alarms he had set last night. He wouldn't be needing them. It had been a long night with only a few short bursts of fitful sleep. He'd spent most of it in miserable turmoil.

After leaving Maia's the day before, the anger he felt had quickly melted away, leaving behind only pain and fear. When she had called later that night, picking up was not an option. He did not want to lose her, much less face that reality over an impersonal phone call. Derek feared the worst and though he knew his thoughts were irrational, it did not allay his fear of losing the woman he loved.

Reluctantly, he showered and got ready for church. He had set up a meeting with his father before service to discuss the future of the ministry, but now that the day was here, it was just adding to the weight on his shoulders.

By the time he walked into the sanctuary that morning, his palms were sweating at the thought of seeing Maia there. He dreaded the very thought of her going back to Eli.

As he stood outside his father's office, he took a deep breath and composed himself. He had discussed his decision with Maia a few days ago and he was sure about what he wanted to do. His certainty did not make this day any easier though. He said a quick prayer before pushing the door.

Across town, Maia awoke to pain. The tightness in her abdomen was an unwanted alarm clock. She sat up in the bed, struggling to breathe through the pain. This was easily the most painful contraction she'd experienced since becoming pregnant. It felt different from the others. Immediately, she began to panic as she realized she could be in labor. There were still eight days left until her due date. Lily couldn't come yet! The pain quickly dissipated though, and so did her frantic thoughts.

Reminding herself that she was as prepared as she could be, Maia prayed for grace and safety. About half an hour later, Lily began her usual morning movements and Maia breathed a sigh of relief. Her baby was okay. Since no more contractions had followed the first in the subsequent hours, she decided to get ready for church. She had to talk to Derek.

Destiny picked her up shortly after and they made their way to church. Maia wasted no time in searching for Derek. She made sure to sit in the lower level instead of her usual balcony seat. As her eyes scanned the auditorium, she found him on the platform, guitar in hand. Even from her considerable distance in the congregation, she could see the exhaustion written all over his face. Maia just wanted to be in his arms, to let him know that he was the only man she wanted.

She waited anxiously for the service to come to an end and as soon as Carl finished the closing prayer, she left Destiny and made a beeline to the base of the stage where Derek was now descending. With his guitar slung over his shoulder in its case, his foot landed on the last step before he noticed her presence. His eyes collided with hers and without asking, she could see every emotion play across his face: fear, sadness, and finally resignation.

"Hey," she greeted.

He hesitated for a minute before responding. "Hey."

"Can we talk please?"

"I don't think that's necessary. I get it Maia. Being with him is certainly a whole lot simpler than being with me. I get it."

"You don't get anything, my handsome doofus. We need to talk." Taking his hand, she led him through the door adjacent to the stage. It could have been the door to Timbuktu for all she knew, but as she stepped through, it opened to a long corridor lined with doors on each side.

"Do you even know where you're going?" Derek intoned, squeezing her hand softly to bring her to a stop.

Turning around, she rested her hand on his chest and shook her head. "I have no idea but we need to talk. Which one of these rooms can we use?"

He pointed to a room two doors down on their left so she waddled to the door. As it closed behind them, she turned on her heel to face Derek, not even taking in that it was the band's prep room.

"Why weren't you taking my calls?" she inquired defiantly, folding her arms and resting them on her rounded stomach.

"Because I wasn't ready to hear what you wanted to tell me." His shoulders slumped and he hung his head, shaking it slowly.

"And what do you suppose I wanted to tell you?"

Ignoring her question, he replied, "I came by yesterday. I'm not sure if *he* told you."

"He did. I still don't understand why you left and stopped taking my calls."

"He made it pretty clear what was happening. I wasn't about to stick around to be humiliated even more."

"Derek, you idiot. Don't you know that I only want you? From all I've told you of Eli, don't you know better than to trust anything that comes out of his mouth? He found me because I forgot to turn off my location sharing. He came to Texas to bribe me into silence not to try to win me back. Even if he did, D, he didn't stand a chance. I'm yours and I don't want anyone else. You didn't even give me the chance to explain that to you. You just disappeared. I need you to trust me if we're going to make it."

She reached up and framed his face with her hands. Her eyes pleaded with him to believe her.

Derek's eyes searched Maia's as her small hands rested on his cheeks. Never in his life had he wanted to believe someone more. Since meeting her, Maia had proven herself to be trustworthy, honest, and kind. Yet his fear of being hurt again made his stomach tighten. He wanted to take her in his arms, kiss her senseless, and *finally* say the three words that had been on the tip of his tongue since that first afternoon on his porch, but the words caught in his throat.

Immediately, he felt the conviction of the Holy Spirit. He could not and *would not* allow his insecurities to snatch away his happiness. More than that, He would not charge Maia for Jessica's mistakes. It wasn't fair to her.

"I'm sorry, Maia. I'm so sorry. I was so afraid that I would lose you, I let my own insecurities get the better of me."

He covered the hands at his cheeks with his own and held her gaze.

"You've loved me better than I thought possible and you never have to worry about me doubting you again. I promise you that, Sunshine. Can you forgive me?"

Maia's lip trembled as his words washed over her and tears fought their way from her eyes, traveling quickly down her cheeks. "Already done," she whispered, reaching up to link her hands around his neck in a hug.

Relief flooded Derek's entire body. He wrapped his arms around her tightly. Even with a baby bump between them, they fit together like a puzzle. He felt like he could breathe for the first time since yesterday's ordeal and he realized that this is what home felt like. As long as he got to wrap his arms around her like this at the end of each day, he could live anywhere in the world.

"I love you, Maia Miller, more than I believed possible or probable in my lifetime. You and Lily crashed into my life like a ton of bricks and I haven't been the same since. I can't wait to make you mine forever."

She tightened her arms around him. "It's about time, Derek Hunter. I love you too, more than you could ever know."

Derek pressed his lips to her cheek and squeezed her one last time. Her immediate shriek of pain made him jump backward in surprise.

"Oh no! Did I hug you too hard?" His voice was frantic.

"I need to sit," Maia gritted out through the pain.

Derek helped her to a small stuffed leather sofa in the corner of the room and Maia spent a minute breathing through the pain.

"It's a contraction." She breathed out as the pain eased.

"Contraction? As in labor? We've got to get you to the hospital! Is this your first one?" The slew of sentences left his lips in quick succession and he paced up and down the small room in panic. "Let's go. I'll carry you to my car." He held out both hands, palms-up and cradled as if she could just hop into his arms like a baby.

"Slow down, sailor. Take a breath. I had one earlier this morning, but—"

"What are you doing in church if you're in labor?" Derek screeched.

Maia rolled her eyes, accepting that she would not be able to have a decent conversation with him in his current state. "They're still hours apart, D. The doctor said to come in when they're an hour apart at most."

"What should we be doing right now? Are you still in pain?"

"Breathe, Derek. They pass pretty quickly. I'm good now. Des is waiting for me out there."

Maia moved to get up and before she could brace her feet to stand, Derek was at her side, hands at her waist in support.

"Let's get you home."

Derek followed Maia and Destiny to her apartment complex. They all went inside and the two fluttered about, fussing over whether Maia was comfortable. In order to secure some time to think, she requested that Derek put her hospital necessities in his car since he insisted on being the one to take her to the hospital. Destiny, whom she had assigned to tea-making, was now in the kitchen doing so noisily. Maia suspected that she was just as panicked as Derek was, given the frequent clanging of silverware in her kitchen.

Maia finally took a deep breath and calmed herself. They had called the hospital earlier and after some convincing from Derek, the nurse agreed for them to come to the hospital. Maia watched enough birthing videos to know that she would be restricted to eating ice chips for a good many hours until Lily came. Therefore, she delayed their departure by requesting the tea.

Her relief was short-lived though and a little while later, both Derek and Destiny were back, watching her sip her tea like she would explode at any moment. She took her time sipping the warm, fruity beverage until another contraction came. As soon as the pain ended, they packed her in the car despite her protests and headed to the hospital.

Chapter 21

The next few hours passed like lightning despite the pain. As her labor progressed, Derek and Destiny stood on either side of the hospital bed. Derek wiped her forehead and spoke soothing words during her contractions. Meanwhile, Des looked like she might faint.

"I'm never having sex again," Destiny whispered as a particularly bad contraction ended.

Maia chuckled. "I'm not in a position to convince you otherwise," she replied, her breaths coming in short pants.

Soon it was time to push and in spite of her being in the worst pain of her life, Maia felt a superhuman strength enter her that was fueled by the need to finally hold her baby. She zoned out the horrified look on Derek's face and the faint expression Des wore and concentrated solely on following the doctor's instructions.

After half an hour of pushing, a nurse placed her 6 pounds, 2 ounces miracle in her arms and everyone else in the world disappeared. The beautiful, brown eyes looking up at her made the last year of her life worth every bit of hardship she had borne. Lily Anne Miller was here. And she looked just like her mama.

The next month passed in a haze of sleepy exhilaration. Maia loved being Lily's mom. She was the most beautiful baby in the world, Derek and Des agreed. They were both champions. She didn't know how she would have survived a month without their help. They both showed up daily to assist. Maia was somehow even more in love with Derek than she had been a month ago. Without a doubt, he loved Lily like she was his own flesh and blood. Every evening after work, he came over and held Lily, fed her, burped her, and spoke a baby language that Lily seemed to understand.

Today, both Derek and Destiny were at her apartment and the two took turns holding Lily as Maia took a little time to get herself together. She took a relaxing, unhurried shower before donning pajamas and returning to the living room with the others. As she entered, she found them whispering conspiratorially on the couch. Lily gurgled over Derek's shoulder as he mumbled something to Destiny.

"Am I going to be a part of this top-secret mission you two are planning?" Maia asked, strolling into the room. They both startled at her words, looking like deer in headlights.

Destiny shot up from the couch. "It's been a long day," she said stretching. "I better get going. I forgot there's-a thing-I need to do."

Maia squinted, her eyes flitting from Destiny to Derek and then back again. "What's going on? You two are acting weird."

"It's nothing," Derek piped up. "Des was just telling me that she needed to prep for some depositions that she has tomorrow."

"Yes!" Des exclaimed, her voice a decibel too loud. "Just let me get one last snuggle in before I go." She said, reaching for Lily. She held the baby close to her chest, closing her eyes and taking a deep sniff of Lily's neck.

"Are you sniffing my baby?" Maia asked, laughing. She perched on the arm of the couch, watching Destiny in bemusement.

"Yes. She smells like heaven. Don't you, Lily-Mily?" Destiny replied, holding the infant away from her to ask the question. Lily's face contorted before finally settling into what looked like a smile. Destiny squealed.

"She smiled!"

"That's definitely gas," Maia and Derek said at the same time, before bursting into laughter.

"First of all, you two need to use your telepathic abilities for something that's actually beneficial, like a game show or the lottery." Des spoke the words as she handed Lily back to Derek.

"Destiny, only you would tell a preacher to play the lottery," he replied with mock consternation.

"You know me by now, Hunter," Destiny said with a shrug and a smile.

"That I do," Derek replied distractedly, his eyes focused on the baby. Lily had the man wrapped around her little finger already. Maia knew there would be no hope for him once their daughter could talk. He would spoil her rotten.

"Well, that's my cue. I bid you both, *adieu*." Des packed up her things before saying a final goodbye.

As she left, Derek rose to his feet with Lily over his shoulder. Spit up from earlier had soaked through his shirt on the same shoulder but Lily cooed, seemingly satisfied. He walked over to her crib and laid her down before turning to Maia with an anxious look.

"What's wrong?" she asked worriedly. Derek ambled over to her, taking her hands in his.

"Every day that I come here, my heart is so full. I love you and Lily more than I love myself and I couldn't ask for anything more than you two." He brushed his lips softly against the back of her hand.

Maia shivered as his lips grazed her skin and tilted her head up to look at him.

"It devastates me when I have to leave at the end of each day. I don't want to leave anymore, Mai. I know without a shadow of a doubt that I want to spend the rest of my life loving you and our beautiful little girl."

Derek knelt down, fishing a small, black velvet box from his pocket. Maia stood in shock, her eyes widening and her hand landing on her lips in surprise.

"With that being said, Maia Corinne Miller, will you do me the honor of being my wife?"

Tears welled in Maia's eyes and she dropped to her knees with him. It was the perfect proposal. She'd never been drawn to fanfare. This ordinary day had been filled with so much love. It was a perfect representation of what she wanted for the rest of her life: a family and home filled with warmth and love.

She nodded through tears, taking his face in her hands and planting a watery kiss on his lips.

"Of course, I'll marry you, D. I'd like nothing more."

Derek placed the cushion cut diamond ring on her finger and they stood and embraced each other for what felt like a blissful eternity. Maia relished the moment. It was more than her heart could take.

"When are we having this wedding, Mr. Hunter?" She asked eventually. Her arms tightened around him.

"How about tomorrow?" he grinned.

"How about next week?" Maia countered.

Derek pulled back to look at her. "Are you serious?"

She nodded nervously.

He moved a stray lock of hair from her face and kissed her cheek. "I want you to have the wedding you deserve, Sunshine. Decorations, a reception…the works. You deserve a beautiful wedding day."

If possible, her love for him grew in that moment.

"I don't need all that. I want you and Lily and as many kids as we'll have. That's what I want. Forever with you. And I want forever to start as soon as possible."

"Aht, aht! You're not about to have me crying in here, woman." Derek fanned his glassy eyes. He took a moment to compose himself as emotions overtook him. "I don't need any convincing, Sunshine. I'm sure I can find someone to make our dreams come true at short notice."

"I think God already did that, babe." Maia beamed.

"That He did. That He certainly did."

"Wait, is this what you and Des were talking about earlier?" she asked, suddenly remembering their strange behavior.

Derek grinned, "Yeah. I needed to get you alone so I could do this. I've been carrying the ring around for a couple of weeks, waiting for the perfect moment. I think I realized today that no moment would ever be perfect enough, so I just took the leap of faith."

"It *was* perfect, D. You have no idea just how perfect it was."

Derek kissed his fiancée again and they both stood embracing, hearts full, in awe of an awesome God.

Chapter 22

It was as beautiful as anyone's wedding day should be. The air was crisp, but the sky was blue and there wasn't a cloud to be seen in the sky. Derek's property had been transformed into a "rustic, bohemian swirl" according to their wedding planner, Onri. The small, willowy biracial man had worked a miracle in a week. He was eccentric, but looking at how beautifully his backyard had been transformed, Derek could easily say it was money well spent. The only responsibility the couple had in the preparations was fitting their clothes. Onri had tackled everything else, for which Derek was grateful.

As he stepped out onto the grass of his backyard, he bent to give Zeke a playful rub on his head. The dog lay on a patch of grass behind the wedding guests, completely unimpressed by the hoopla. Zeke wagged his tail as Derek petted him, but immediately resumed his nonchalant review of the day's proceedings. Derek straightened, leaving the dog and walking up the aisle to the altar. As he turned to face their guests, he smiled and waved nervously. There was a collective chuckle and then James gave a loud hoot of encouragement.

"My lad's getting hitched!"

Lian swatted James' thigh in admonition. Derek grinned at his friend. The guests erupted into laughter again.

He looked at their twenty friends and family gathered to support them and he thanked God. The Lord's faithfulness was unmatched. His eyes landed on Clarissa sitting in the second row and he winked at her. She hadn't been able to afford a flight on short notice, but had insisted on them going ahead with the wedding. He knew Maia had been disappointed so he managed to conspire with Clarissa to fly her in for the occasion. Hopefully, it would make Maia's day that much more special. He adjusted the bow tie at his neck and waited impatiently for his soon-to-be wife to walk down the aisle.

Upstairs in a guest bedroom, Maia sat in front of the mirror as Des pinned a beautiful white and pearl hair vine to the base of the bride's chignon. Her makeup was simple yet beautiful as was her straight, lace wedding gown.

"Well, that's that. Time to get married, girl." Des' eyes met hers in the mirror and Maia's eyes welled with tears.

"Oh no you don't!" Des squealed, running to the bed to get a tissue for her. "You'll mess up the makeup I worked hard on." She rested her arm on her hips and met Maia's eyes again.

"Thank you for everything, Des. You're the best friend I've ever had and I wouldn't be here if it weren't for you. Thank you for reminding me that I was worthy of love even when I didn't feel like I was."

"Oh hush!" Des fanned her hand in the air. "That's what friends do. Now let's get you downstairs before that man drags you down there himself."

Maia nodded and they made their way downstairs. Destiny left Maia at the door that led to the porch and scurried down the aisle to take her seat next to Luke at the front. She gave a thumbs up as a cue to Onri who stood by the sound system and he started the music.

The guests rose to their feet and turned toward the bride, but Maia saw none of that. Her eyes were locked with her tall, handsome almost-husband. He smiled at her and she melted inside. Every time she looked at him, she was reminded of God's kindness to her. This little slice of heaven was undoubtedly His kindness.

As she made her way up the aisle, her eyes searched the seats for her baby and she found her in Coretta's arms, bundled up and sleeping soundly. She felt like her heart might burst from happiness. Her eyes were traveling back to Derek when familiar silver hair caught her eye. She did a double take before her eyes confirmed that she was in fact looking at Mimi, sitting in the second row to her left. Maia stopped dead in her tracks and leaned down to give her grandmother a tight hug.

"How?" Maia whispered in her ear.

"That man will do anything to make you happy, baby."

Maia could not hold the tears back any longer. She released Mimi and hurried to the altar where Carl and Derek stood. She didn't want another hour to go by without her being this man's wife. As they stood and faced each other, Derek lifted a finger to wipe her tears away. He mouthed an "I love you" as Carl began the ceremony.

Their short reception was held under a sailcloth tent set up just yards from the ceremony. They ate together, laughed, and enjoyed one another's company. Maia and Derek mingled, making sure to spend time with each guest.

As they approached Des and Luke, Maia's eyes pierced the older man's own. Her friend made introductions and Maia waited for warning bells to fire off as she assessed the tall and handsome man. None came. He seemed genuine with blue eyes that held considerable sadness. Luke looked like a man who had lived through more pain than anyone should have to bear. It sat in the slight hunch of his shoulders and the tentative way he smiled, like he was afraid to be happy. Nevertheless, Maia could not walk away without offering him a sobering warning, "Treat my friend right or you'll have to answer to us. She deserves to be treated like a queen so treat her as such."

Derek and Des stood quietly in the awkward aftermath of her words, but Luke's eyes met hers boldly.

"I got off to a rocky start but I promise you *and* her," he announced, his eyes drifting to Destiny's, "I'll treat her the way she deserves, for as long as she'll have me."

Maia nodded in acknowledgment. She still wasn't sure about the man, but she trusted her friend's judgment and as it always did, time would tell.

"Thank you for always having my back, Mrs. Hunter," Des said, pulling her into a brief embrace.

"Always."

Derek gave Maia's waist a light squeeze, a sure way of telling her it was time to move on.

"It was nice to meet you, Luke. Y'all enjoy the rest of the reception, now," Derek said politely, steering Maia away from the couple.

"In a hurry?" Maia asked as he led her in the direction of his parents.

"Yes. I'd like to spend some alone time with my wife." His hand drifted to the small of her back and he stopped to give her a kiss.

Maia chuckled. "Let's go talk to your parents and then we're kicking these people out," she winked.

As they approached Carl and Coretta, Maia immediately held her hands out to take Lily. Coretta handed her over, smiling knowingly.

"New mamas…" she quipped, looking at Carl.

"Welcome to the family, Maia. We're elated to have you be part of the Hunter clan," Carl piped up, giving her a brief hug. He turned to Derek. "I'm proud of you, son. I was disappointed you turned down the pastorate, but I admire your courage and wisdom in doing so. I wanted you to take the post, but that was not God's will for you and I appreciate your honesty. Pastor Wilson and his wife have been with our church from the ground up. I know that with Rose by his side, they're more than capable of taking over. They've got amazing plans for the people of Turnpeake and a vision I can get behind. I guess what I'm saying is thank you for following your purpose. It led Coretta and I to the Lord's choice instead of my own."

Carl pulled his son into an aggressive hug, giving him three solid pats on the back. Maia saw Derek quickly wipe his eyes and she smiled. He had carried so much guilt from turning down his father's offer. Carl's words must have lifted that heavy burden.

"Love you, pop." Derek hugged his dad again and then embraced his mother. "Thank you for supporting us," he added, taking Maia's hand in his. "We appreciate it more than you know."

His parents beamed at them.

"Now, go give these people a first dance before you put us all out," Carl laughed, reaching for Lily.

Derek led his wife to a small patch of grass in the center of the tent and they began to sway to a familiar song. Her hands linked around his neck and his own rested comfortably on her waist. She leaned into him and breathed in his familiar scent. It was intoxicating yet comforting. She smiled up at her husband. "I love you forever, Derek Hunter."

"And I love you forever and a day, Maia Hunter."

He kissed his bride and their eyes drifted to their precious gift of a daughter. Derek pulled her closer and they cherished that moment of utter perfection, relishing their little piece of heaven on earth.

Epilogue

—•—

Three years later

"Mama, Jesse broke my doll!" Lily presented the headless and miniature figure of a woman to her mother, who sat resting in a wicker chair on the porch. The little girl stood pouting, with the doll's body in one hand and its head in the next.

"I'm sorry sweetie. I'm sure your brother didn't mean to do it. Let's see if we can fix her," Maia replied, trying to placate her strong-willed three-year-old. She was the absolute cutest little girl to walk the planet and no one could tell her mother any different. Maia reconnected the caramel-complexioned doll and handed it back to her daughter.

"See? Good as new!" She was barely able to kiss Lily's chubby cheeks before she darted off to play with the tiny doll-decapitator who was now chasing a butterfly around the backyard. His little one year old feet were moving at lightning speed. As usual, he had disrobed and was wearing nothing but a diaper. Lily joined him in his pursuit of the big, yellow insect and they giggled together at its elusive fluttering.

"Hey Sunshine."

Maia's eyes shot up to see her husband standing in the doorway. "You're back!" she squealed and jumped up from the wicker chair to embrace him. He pressed his lips to hers and squeezed her tightly.

"Yeah, the conference finished ahead of schedule so I caught the earliest flight out of Denver. I'm never accepting another speaking engagement at a week-long conference again. Ever," he emphasized.

"Derek Hunter," Maia scolded, "I'm sure you helped the hundreds of non-profit leaders who attended. I'm also sure you'll help hundreds more if asked."

"Well, next time I'm bringing y'all with me. I think a few hours is my limit for being away from you. A week was unreasonably difficult," he returned, his hands roving her body like a starved man. Maia smiled up at him flirtatiously before poking him in the ribs.

"*That's* what got us in this predicament," she said, rubbing her four-month-pregnant baby bump. "Speaking of which, your second son has been treating my navel like a punching bag all week."

"I'm sorry baby. He probably missed me too," Derek grinned.

"Daddy!" Lily screamed at the top of her lungs, dashing up the porch steps to her father. Derek wasted no time in scooping her into his arms. Her little hands wrapped around his neck and she rested her head on his shoulder. "I missed you, Daddy."

"I missed you too, princess. I missed you so much." He hugged her tightly. Derek loved all his children, but his daughter held a special place in his heart. Lily had made him a father, and legally adopting her two years ago, had been a natural decision. She was his daughter, through and through.

Zeke, who had been sleeping next to Maia's feet, whipped his head up. His ears perked up as Lily squealed, but the commotion was not enough to justify further investigation so he put his head back down. He wagged his tail briefly before drifting off to sleep again.

Jesse, who had abandoned his quest for the butterfly, now stood at his father's feet, arms outstretched. Derek bent down and picked him up with his free arm.

He hugged the children to himself tightly. His family was his heartbeat. They were his home and it felt *so* good to be home again. Closing his eyes, Derek felt like he could finally breathe again for the first time since he'd left a week ago.

"Let's head inside. Daddy brought surprises for everyone," he announced, winking at Maia. The children screamed in excitement and Derek ushered his wife inside to the kitchen, putting the squirming kids on the floor. They immediately dashed towards the wrapped toys and began tearing the wrapping papers off.

"And you, my beautiful, sweet, incredible wife," he began, turning towards Maia, "I know our anniversary isn't for another eight hours, but I wanted to give you one of your gifts early."

Derek pulled a jewelry box from his pocket and opened it to reveal a beautiful, shimmering, rose gold charm bracelet. There were three charms hanging from it already: a miniature family of five that he'd had custom-made, a cross, and the logo of his wife's non-profit. She'd started the shelter two years ago and together they had built a thriving haven for struggling single mothers.

Maia pressed her hand to her chest as she caught sight of the charms. Tears welled in her eyes. "Thank you, babe. This is the best gift I've ever gotten," she whispered, as he clasped the jewelry around her wrist.

"You say that every year," Derek chuckled.

"That's because you outdo yourself *every year.*"

"Let's hope I can keep it up."

"I'm sure you will. I've gotten you something amazing too, but I'm afraid you'll have to wait until tomorrow to get it," Maia giggled, knowing he'd be absolutely ecstatic about the courtside basketball tickets she had secured for them.

"The suspense…" he gasped and they both laughed.

"I love you, Derek Hunter, mind, body and soul."

"I love you too, Sunshine. Cheers to one more year of forever." He dipped his head to claim her lips with a passionate kiss. It wasn't long before their little minions interrupted, though. Apparently, assembling the new train set he'd gotten them was more important than kissing their mama.

Derek and Maia parted reluctantly and joined their exuberant children on the floor. Tackling the task together, they made light work of the assembly and spent hours playing with Lily and Jesse. After bathing the children and putting them to bed that night, they breathed a collective sigh of relief. As they closed the door to the kids' room, Derek's arm roped around his wife's shoulders and he embraced her from behind. Maia pressed herself into his warmth, allowing her body to melt into his.

"So, Mrs. Hunter, what should we do now?" Derek asked, dipping his head to kiss the soft, smooth skin at her neck.

"Well," Maia whispered. "I say we celebrate."

She turned in his arms and kissed him deeply. Then, taking his hand, she led him down the hallway.

"Gotta love a woman who knows what she wants," Derek said with a low rumble of laughter as she led him into the bedroom. He closed the door softly behind him and Maia turned hooded eyes toward him. "Well, let's get to celebrating, Sunshine," Derek continued, scooping her into his arms and taking her to the bed.

Maia laughed breathlessly, wrapping her arms around his neck. "I love you forever, Derek Hunter." She said the words as her head touched the pillow and her arms reached for him.

"And I love *you* forever, Mrs. Hunter," he answered, joining her. "But I've done enough talking. It's time for me to show you…"

Stay tuned for the next book in the Breaking the Blueprint Series titled, *"Divine Destiny"*.